Issue 10 Winter 2017/18

Science fiction magazine from Scotland

ISSN 2059-2590
ISBN 978-1-9997002-4-9

Shoreline of Infinity is available in digital or print editions.
Submissions of fiction, art, reviews, poetry, non-fiction are welcomed:
visit the website to find out how to submit.

www.shorelineofinfinity.com

Publisher
Shoreline of Infinity Publications / The New Curiosity Shop
Edinburgh
Scotland
211117

Contents

Cover: Dave Alexander

Dave Alexander was born in Glasgow in a dark, frightening epoch before the invention of computers. His biggest claim to fame were the two front covers he painted for DC Thomson's *Starblazer* series of comics. He was instrumental in launching Scotland's first adult humour comic book *Electric Soup*, in 1989. He was one of the team who launched *Northern Lightz* – Scotland's first underground comic book, which also featured science fiction themed stories. Dave works in Glasgow from his own studio, producing a wide range of illustrative work.

Editorial Team

Co-founder, Editor & Editor-in-Chief:
Noel Chidwick

Co-founder, Art Director:
Mark Toner

Deputy Editor & Poetry Editor:
Russell Jones

Reviews Editor:
Iain Maloney

Assistant Editor & First Reader:
Monica Burns

Copy editors:
Iain Maloney, Russell Jones, Monica Burns

Extra thanks to:
Caroline Grebbell, M Luke McDonell, Katy Lennon, Chris Kelso and many others.

First Contact

www.shorelineofinfinity.com

contact@shorelineofInfinity.com

Twitter: @shoreinf

and on Facebook

Pull Up a Log

We've reached double figures. In case you hadn't realised you are holding issue number **10** in your hands. Darn it, we're going to pause on our laurels for a few words.

We've published around 100 stories – mainly from new and emerging writers; 43 poems from 20 poets, and we've illustrated the magazine with the work of about 30 artists. We've published dozens of reviews, many interviews, columns and with SF Caledonia, we've dusted off a selection of early science fiction from some fine Scottish writers. To top it off, in this issue we celebrate the winners of our first flash-fiction competition: all hail Matthew Castle, SK Farrell and Marija Smits.

In partnership with the Edinburgh International Book Festival we have also published a special issue which features some stunning contributions from some world renowned writers.

We've brought out some other publications too – feel free to explore our website for details.

We have also brought live science fiction to audiences with Event Horizon, our monthly mix of words, music, drama and other science fictional performances. We've notched up 26 events so far.

Not too shabby from a team that's been going for just under 3 years. And that's the key word: team. It is a privilege to work with such a fine bunch of talented enthusiasts, some listed on the facing page, who have worked with Mark and me to shape *Shoreline of Infinity*.

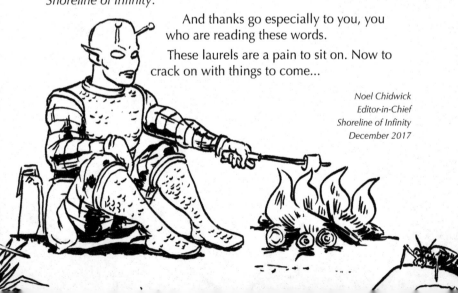

And thanks go especially to you, you who are reading these words.

These laurels are a pain to sit on. Now to crack on with things to come...

Noel Chidwick
Editor-in-Chief
Shoreline of Infinity
December 2017

Little Freedoms

Ephiny Gale

Art: M Luke McDonnell

The room is cylindrical, metal, no doors or windows. Nine of us stand in a circle, not touching, but spread your arms and you'd hit someone. I think I could lie flat in here without brushing the walls, but not by much.

The ceiling hatch above us locks shut with a scrape. We examine faces, muscles, body fat. I've seen six of these women before; two are complete strangers. We do not trade names or origin stories. We go around the circle and we say what we miss most from the outside:

Chocolate, Music, Flowers, Cigarettes, Hot Chips, Internet, Guns, Privacy.

I am Hot Chips. Privacy says hers while staring mournfully at the circular grate in the floor, and I think *oh, she must be new.*

When I was brand new I'd said "My Dog" thinking that was safe, and someone had laughed – not unkindly – and said, "Jeez, at least say your bitch."

The girl to my right asks, "So where are we going?" and there's a flurry of overconfident suggestions from those I assume got in through the physical trials. On the metal floor, every little step sounds like the smack of a frying pan. None of these women can know which terrain we're headed to. We've been told *You Must Not Assault One Another*, otherwise their disagreement may have turned violent.

Four of us are keeping our mouths shut, including me. I assume we're the four who got in the other way – 'The Lottery' – though it's not random at all. How much can you give up in a month? Food, sleep, shelter, dignity?

6

When there's a lull in the argument, Privacy points out a dollar-sized hole in the centre of the ceiling, releasing a single drop of water every two seconds, which falls through the middle of our tiny room and down through the floor grate. "Maybe we're not going anywhere," she says.

This is met with the obligatory smirks and laughter. Still, what feels like about twenty minutes has passed and nothing has happened, and many of us are fiddling with our shirt buttons, our fingernails, with the black bracelets locked on each of our wrists ("WIN YOUR FREEDOM" printed in Helvetica, light grey).

Once about thirty minutes have passed, there's an ascending chime like *the 7:15 train has been delayed* and a strip around the top of the cylinder hisses into pixelated life: *YOU MUST NOT FIDGET*. It's lit up for a couple of seconds, and then the same chime plays in *descending* order and it's gone.

There is laughter again, the most there's been, but now everyone's hands are motionless at their sides, or on their hips, or clasped in front of them. "This the big endurance test?" calls someone with muscles. "What a fucking piece of piss!"

Of course, when you're not allowed to do something you instantly need to do it a hundred times as much. My scalp, which felt fine seconds ago, prickles as if covered in lice. Itches blister down the sides of my neck, my wrist, above my eye. I trap my hands between the wall and my bottom and try to distract myself.

The others are arguing over whether this is the real challenge or not. I can see them flinching and wriggling every so often, as if to shrug off a troublesome insect. I am concentrating on my breathing.

My newfound desire to scratch my nose is shocking. If someone else raked their nails down my face, that wouldn't break the rules, would it? I am not desperate enough to share this secret yet.

The bug-eyed blonde on the floor – Flowers, I think, and maybe Melinda – starts complaining quietly about how much it feels like spiders are crawling over her skin. She knows a lot about spiders, too; she mentions several different breeds and the technical terms for the different segments of their legs. The others keep telling her to shut up, but Flowers keeps going, staring catatonically and moaning about rubbing her whole body against tree bark.

Eventually a girl with orange dreadlocks looks acutely nauseous, hauls Flowers up by the collar and raises her free hand in a fist. Flowers gasps and her eyes bug out like one of those goldfish.

At the last moment the fist uncurls and morphs into a middle finger salute instead.

Released, Flowers sinks back into the wall and smiles bashfully – "I'm sorry, Chocolate, did I upset you?" – but then her eyes darken and there's no confusion as to her innocence. When Chocolate turns her back, Flowers is up like a shot, parting the orange dreadlocks and blowing a single definitive breath on the back of Chocolate's neck.

It's more than enough. Chocolate leaps a foot in the air, scratching her neck with her fingernails like she's trying to rip the skin off. A pitch-black, translucent arm reaches through the metal wall and closes around Chocolate's wristband, and the whole 5'10" of her is yanked out of the room before the floor has even stopping vibrating from her jump.

Silence from the eight of us in the slightly-more-spacious cylinder. My eyes float slowly across from where Chocolate disappeared to the grate where Flowers is standing.

She looks completely serious. "Piece of piss, right?" she says.

YOU MUST NOT STAND.

There is no doubt anymore. This is our endurance test, and it will get easier and easier to lose, and we will be in here for as long as it takes.

When the second instruction flashes up, accompanied by the chime, we all sink to the ground almost in unison. There's not enough room for everyone to stretch out their legs at once, which is cause for some squabbling, but a rough hierarchy soon establishes itself.

With their legs out: Guns, the pretty Asian with the high-pony, the first to pee over the grate; Music, an athletic black woman with a chin scar; Cigarettes, a white girl who looks almost plump

8

compared to the rest of us; and Flowers, with her legs half-over all the others'.

It's not like you can get far away from Flowers in here, but I'm pleased she's not *right* next to me.

Privacy asks Flowers why she's so desperate to get out – does she have children outside? And there's less laughter than I'm expecting, but all I can think is *new, new, God, you're so new.* Flowers says it's none of their business, but isn't that so stereotypical, that a woman needs to be a mother to throw someone else under the bus – can't she just want to free herself more than some strangers?

The room actually seems to warm to Flowers after that. Privacy climbs carefully over the outstretched legs and crouches over the grate, tilting her head to catch the ceiling drips on her tongue. I glance around and see a few women silently calculating whether to stop her – if they can hold her down until she's no longer a threat of any kind – but no-one moves.

We take it in turns to crouch under the drip and almost drink enough. While I'm sitting there, hurting my neck and seizing up my limbs, someone yells, "No camels!" which means I'm done for now.

Two or three hours have passed and it must be dark outside. The girl to my right, Internet, who's said barely more than I have, presses her lips to my ear and says, "Help me with something and I'll make it worth your while." I study her bony face, dark eyes, freckles... And nod.

She smiles and holds up the shoelaces she's pulled free. We're all in new uniforms for this and I feel stupid for not registering the laces earlier. "I want to sleep," she whispers. "But I'm afraid I'll itch. Can you tie up my fingers?"

I thread the laces between her digits and knot them so her fingers stay apart, then tie her hands together with the excess length. Some of the other women make bondage jokes, and though I think a couple understand the actual purpose they're not sharing out loud.

"You'll scratch my nose?" I ask, and she does, one long, firm scratch down both sides with her awkward bundle of hands.

"That's the bonus," she says, but doesn't elaborate.

Internet props herself against me, back to back, hands in lap, and might be napping as far as I know. The others aren't yelling, exactly, but there's a lively discussion about whether it's like this every year. The losers aren't allowed to mention the competition afterward, and the winner never comes back, of course.

I couldn't sleep with all that noise.

At one point Flowers unbuttons her shirt, folds it neatly and tucks it under her bottom. Everyone stares at her bare chest with various degrees of subtlety, because there are *actual* flowers there – tattoos of orchids stretching from her waist to the top of one breast, purple and yellow like permanent bruises.

It should make her more vulnerable, but Flowers wears it like armour and the group seems to treat it as such.

In the wake of this, Guns leans over and sticks her tongue inside Privacy's ear, and Privacy lets out a horrified gasp but doesn't jump to her feet like Guns obviously wants her to. I wait to see if The Powers That Be consider this assault, but apparently not, and thankfully Guns doesn't follow it with anything more extreme.

A couple more hours pass without incident and the group seems to conclude that now, in the early stages, is a useful time to get some sleep. I've agreed since Internet slumped against my back, but I can't let my eyes close. I'm a violent sleeper, the kind that steals the covers and kicks shins and tosses like a suffocating fish.

Some of the other women get shoe laces tied around their fingers. One by one, threats are issued or goodnights whispered and eyelids shut around the circle. Then there's only Music, Flowers and me awake and staring at one another.

My legs are aching by now, and one of them has suffered pins and needles for the last half hour. I twist carefully on the floor and stretch my legs into the air in the middle of the circle, careful not to touch the sleepers. While I massage the feeling back into my calves, I can see Flowers grinning at me from the corner of my eye.

Flowers is making hand puppets at me. I can't tell what they are, exactly, but they change rapidly and are surprisingly animate. I force my face to stay blank, impassive. Eventually she cocks her head like *poor dumb bitch* and opens her mouth as if to scream.

Silence. She shuts her mouth again, then opens it and takes a deep breath.

More silence. She does this a third time, and it really looks like she's going to screw up her face and shriek, but Music shoves her own shirt in Flowers' mouth and ties it firmly behind her blonde head.

Flowers jerks against the wall and reaches up for the ties, picking at the knot for a second before realising that's an awful lot like fidgeting. She glares at Music for a straight hour after that, and Music stares back for a lot of it. Allowing your competition to sleep seems a strange tactic to me, but perhaps Music just hates Flowers. Or loves the silence. Or has a tiny, fragile alliance, like mine with Internet.

We sit there for a while longer until Flowers gradually retrieves her legs from the middle of the circle and picks her way, hunched and Gollum-like, over to me. She unfolds something navy and red-brown between us – her shirt, wet with menstrual blood – and manages to grin at me around her gag.

I open my mouth to protest, but she pivots to the girl on my left instead.

I realise I don't know this girl, and I don't remember the thing she misses most – I don't think I even heard it in the first place. And now Flowers is draping the bloody shirt over her head, and the wet part's all over her sleeping face.

Flowers sits back down and I'm frozen to the wall, and it's not like this is the worst thing I've ever seen, far from it, but it's so *silent* and *cold* and *easy* when getting here in the first place was so damn *hard*.

The ascending chime goes off, and it is *loud*.

Several things happen at once. No-name next to me wakes up with a face full of cotton and blood, and kind of a half-sob and staggers to her feet and gets dragged through the wall.

The rest are frantically blinking themselves awake and trying to focus on their new instructions, which, incidentally, read *YOU MUST NOT SLEEP.*

And Internet is struggling towards the grate, pulling down her pants awkwardly with her tied hands, and rocking back too far at the last moment...

She pees on everyone but me.

Internet sits back down and doesn't apologise, because what is there to say, and women don't generally pee in a 180-degree arc by accident.

There are shouts of outrage and swearing and clearly suppressed wriggling from the other prisoners. Privacy looks like she's going to throw up, and I expect her to throw in the towel at this point but she doesn't move.

Instead, Cigarettes is the one flailing and shaking her legs to try and get the piss off them, and bounding to her feet and the urine's running down her ankles and then there's a translucent hand around her bracelet and she's gone.

Guns, Privacy, Music and Flowers are all taking off their soiled shoes and trousers and I think I had better, too, so I don't draw attention to my relative cleanliness. They toss their trousers at Internet, who is soon sitting in a pile of dirty cotton, and their shoes in a cluster over the grate so they're not eliminated for actually battering the woman. Music mimes several different ways of ending Internet's life, includes slicing her jugular, wrists, hanging, stabbed in the guts... Music has her thumbs in her underwear and I think she might go and return Internet's 'favour' but Guns mouths "Later" and the room is silent for a bit.

Privacy has started crying in that way where the tears drop but the rest of your face looks normal. Guns leans over and licks them off her cheeks with some comment about water conservation. Through her makeshift gag, Flowers starts humming a familiar tune that I haven't heard for years and can't quite put my finger on. It's a children's song, one of those ones that keeps repeating over and over.

"It's that bear song," says Internet, slowly shifting the peed-on trousers away from her and onto the grate. And of course it is, that song about a bunch of bears in a bed and they all roll over and fall out one by one until it's just the little bear left and I've forgotten what happens then, if anything. Flowers is still humming and Guns calls her a sociopath.

And then there are six of us, and there's almost enough space to be comfortable, and there's wakefulness stretching before us like the desert – all the way to the horizon.

The cylinder is truly unpleasant now. The smell of drying urine is impossible to ignore, as is the hunger gnawing at my stomach. It's easy to imagine the hunger as a seventh person, expanding around us until she fills all the empty space. It's going to be one of us Lottery girls next, I'm sure, quitting just for the relief of a proper meal.

When the chime sounds again, the pile of trousers has moved and Privacy is squatting tenuously under the drip. Flowers scuttles along the floor and drags Privacy back towards the wall by her biceps, where Privacy flails and collides with Music in a muddle of limbs. Flowers claims the spot over the grate just as *YOU MUST NOT TOUCH* blinks to life above us.

I watch the conflict flash desperately over Music's face. There's barely time to extract herself, so instead she throws Privacy aside. Privacy's a tall woman so it has to be a big push, but the force slams Privacy's arms and forehead against the metal floor and there's no doubt about the pain involved.

The descending tone finishes and Music's bottom lip quivers. Then there's a hand around her wrist, and she sinks back into the wall like it's liquid and disappears.

Flowers is kneeling on the grate, head tipped back and catching the water happily on her gag. The ramifications of this slowly register: as long as we're not allowed to touch her, and as long as Flowers doesn't move, she's effectively cut off our water supply. None of us can reach it without standing or risking touching her.

"Fuck you, Melinda," says Guns, and we watch Privacy pick herself up like reassembling a doll. She isn't bleeding or crying, but there's a hardness to her face I haven't seen before. I suppose she might have a concussion.

"No-one would blame you for leaving," Guns tells her. "*That* kind of hurt – it's not part of the rules."

Privacy leans herself gingerly against the wall and doesn't answer.

"Alright," says Guns, now addressing everyone. "Just remember that this could be a lot worse. Forgotten what it's like outside? If you can't survive in here you'll have trouble out there. You can't die in prison."

Internet tucks her hands between her thighs. "You can die anywhere," she says.

And it's tempting. It's so tempting. How much I want to scratch, stand and stretch, drink and eat my fill, sleep and feel someone's hands on me. To recover those little freedoms. I have lost all sense of time in this place. *How long how long how long.*

My tired eyes rest on Flowers and an idea sparks.

For the first time since we were locked in here, I shift from my designated spot in the circle and crawl around to the opposite wall. Guns and Internet swing their legs over to accommodate me.

I peel a couple of pair of trousers from the soiled pile, trying to ignore their dampness, and tie both right legs together at the ankles; they'll stretch out to almost four legs' worth of length now. The knot is as secure as I can make it.

I keep hold of one end of the trouser-rope and slide the other end in Guns and Internet's direction. They both eye it for a second, and then Guns gives me the ghost of a smirk and picks up the cotton ankle I've offered. We pull the rope almost tight and it stretches neatly across the diameter of the circle.

Flowers still has her face to the sky and looks oblivious. I feel a delirious burst of satisfaction at the back of my skull.

Guns mouths *one, two, three* and then we swing the rope in an arc over Flower's head. It catches her mid-thigh and we hook it under her arms before she can retaliate. We jerk the rope backwards and up, and in a deliciously similar manner to what she did to Privacy, Flowers is yanked off the grate and pinned up against the wall.

For a moment Flowers seems frozen with terror, but I know her stillness is simply profound control of the game. She doesn't bash her feet against the floor. She doesn't try and untangle her arms; she will touch us if she does, and she will be disqualified. She contents herself by swivelling her head between Guns and myself, administering some of the most withering looks I've seen.

Internet and Privacy tie the last pairs of trousers together – Internet has to remove her own pair for an even number – and between the four of us we manage to tie Flowers' arms to her sides and her knees together. Then we take grateful turns under the drip. One of us could easily monopolise the water again, but there are still several shirts we can tie in knots, and no-one else wants to end up like Flowers.

A little while later, Privacy comes and leans next to me whilst Guns is drinking. "Tell me," she says. "Why no names? No back-stories? Just this one thing you miss. No-one explains properly."

I feel sweaty and self-conscious and exhausted. "I don't know," I mumble. "I guess because those first two don't matter in here. We're never getting the past back. But maybe it's not too much to ask, that one small thing you miss most. Maybe you can get that back, in another life."

I see her nod from the corner of my eye. "Like hot chips?"

I shrug. "It seems a reasonable thing to want."

We smile at each other, just a little, and for a moment the competition is a fraction easier.

Then Guns rocks back onto her ass. She stares at the ceiling – the dry ceiling, the ceiling that is no longer dripping – and we are plunged into the next phase with no ceremony whatsoever.

If time had seemed unwieldy before, now it feels utterly amorphous. Logically, we can't really have been stuck in the cylinder for all that long, but it's suddenly difficult to imagine life outside these few cubic meters. I fight the nearly-overwhelming urge to leave just to reassure myself that other places – other situations – exist.

And even with my churning hunger and sickening exhaustion, it is so *dull* in here. No-one wants to talk without access to water, and this test seems to have reduced itself to *who can sit here the longest*. I wish I was smart enough to think of a way to eliminate the others – I could even justify it as putting them out of their misery – but I can't come up with a thing.

Finally, Flowers starts crashing her heels against the floor, causing great thumps to reverberate throughout the room. They're slow, methodical; no one could accuse her of fidgeting. The others glance amongst themselves to see if they can stop her somehow, but it's not like they can hogtie her. And I am oddly grateful for the interruption, the un-ignorable sound, the vibrations which run up my stiff legs. I feel a rush of absurd affection for Flowers.

But Flowers doesn't stop the banging. Guns and I end up curled on the floor, shirts cushioning our heads and hands muffling our exposed ears. Privacy and Internet seem happier sitting, though there's barely room for them to do otherwise. Guns has two Asian characters tattooed on the underside of her wrists, and I spend a good half hour or so trying to deduce their meaning.

I could ask, of course, but that would ruin the game.

Flowers goes on for so long her heels must be swollen with orchid-bruises. I don't know what makes her snap in the end. But one moment she's bashing the floor, the next she's rolling into Internet, whose jaw drops like Flowers has just slid a knife into her gut.

They leave silently, simultaneously.

I guess Flowers decided she couldn't win. I would've thought she'd take Guns with her, but then Internet's pee has pressed against her skin for the last few eternities. There's a half-dried bloodstain where Flowers was sitting.

I am very, very lucky.

There are just three of us left. Not at all the last three I was expecting. My brain's not working so well anymore. I have the sudden image of the cylinder as a time capsule, and someone digging up our skeletons in a hundred years.

The sign flashes YOU MUST NOT TALK, and clearly, no shits are given.

Something flares in my aching chest. Only two more to beat.

I could actually win.

The next part is a small lifetime. I allow myself to fantasise about my possible freedom. Will they let me sleep and wash and dress before throwing me out, or just take me directly outside, starving and thirsty and half-naked?

I will strip 'til I'm bare and stand in the sun. I will stare at an uninterrupted horizon. I will lick salt and spices from my fingers. I will never take anything for granted again.

The ascending chime, and then YOU MUST NOT MOVE.

Frantic movements as we all try and stretch out onto our backs without touching each other.

We succeed.

Privacy doesn't have anything between her head and the floor; Guns and I will be much more comfortable.

And for the first few minutes, this is better than the nothingness. I am concentrating on not moving. Not moving a millimetre. Of course, no-one can concentrate forever.

My shoulder blades press down against the metal.

I just have to last longer than the others.

I assume the rules are the same as Sleeping Lions or Dead Fish, those games we played as a kid when the adults wanted ten minutes of peace: breathing and blinking are still allowed. We're on our backs so we can still read the pixelated sign, though I can't imagine how our freedom could be restricted further. Our eyes have to be open for that, and so we have to be able to blink.

I think of myself as a corpse. As a mannequin. I am acutely aware of every protesting part of my body. I think of the time I needed my wisdom teeth out, but the teeth were too close to my nerves, and if I'd moved even a millimetre during surgery I would have permanently lost the feeling in my jaw.

So I didn't have that surgery, but I can do this. I am made of fucking *steel*.

There are times when I think *I want to die, I want to die*, but I don't move. I will not move. Not when I've come this far.

A small sound whistles to my right. Guns really must have been comfortable, because she's *snoring*. And then, of course, she's not there anymore.

I think of Privacy. If this was a kinder world, I would sacrifice myself for her, or she would sacrifice herself for me. And things would be hopeful and uplifting and we'd know we'd done the right thing.

But this is not that world.

The chime comes again, for the last time, and it says *YOU MUST NOT BREATHE.*

I hold my breath on the second last note.

I don't know if I can do this. I was a decent swimmer, once upon a time, but that was years ago.

I stare at the ceiling and bite my tongue.

The pressure is building in my stomach, my nose, my throat. It feels like my face is an overfilled balloon, about to burst. Heat crawls up my neck. I think I can see Privacy from the corner of one eye: I just need to hold on longer than her. Just a millisecond longer. Then I can breathe.

Privacy is still lying there. My vision is blurring.

It's involuntary. I can't- I won't-

I take a breath and cry out. It's a tiny cry. There is no energy for tears. My whole body is shaking. I have lost. I will not get to leave. All that, so much for nothing.

I keep expecting to feel a shadowy hand on my wrist, but seconds pass and it never does.

I struggle to my knees. Privacy must know she's won, but she's just lying there. Still motionless. I can't even see her chest rising. *The head blow?*

I crawl across the room and press my fingers to her neck, hold them under her nose.

She really did stop breathing.

I slouch over the grate and stare at nothing in particular. It's awful, it's a tragedy, but mostly all I can think is *I've won, I've won by default* and laugh and laugh inside my head, and it feels like my skin's just peeled off my body and I've been given a fresh, light, clean one.

Beside me, a large panel slides open in the wall and the prison warden steps through, flanked by her usual guards.

"I won," I say, sounding like a small child and not caring.

"No," says the warden. "Geraldine won."

Is that really Privacy's name, I think, numb. *It doesn't fit her.*

I blink at them, feeling like the adults have come home to my messy playroom. "She's dead," I say. "I won."

"You took a breath before she did. You knew the rules. And she's already received her prize; she has her freedom."

The wind is knocked out of me. The guards pick me up and carry me out. I cannot move. I cannot speak. Slowly, I adjust to the world outside the cylinder.

Next year, I think. Next year I'll win.

And in the meantime, little freedoms.

Ephiny's fiction has been published in *GigaNotoSaurus, Aurealis, Daily Science Fiction*, and two Belladonna Publishing anthologies. She has also written a variety of produced stage plays and musicals, several of which have been collected in The Playbook. She is currently working on a short story collection. More at www.ephinygale.com

Sweet Compulsion

Chris Bailey

I believed I was going to turn transmitter and so I left that city. The air there felt solid with message. The dust that whipped up along the baked streets, the water we washed in — everything, glittering with meme.

Receptors... We couldn't help being receptors. Message was so prolific I spent my life scrubbing my skin or sitting in decon, trying to kill it off before it infiltrated me. I felt raw. I didn't want to share Garcia's end. His defences had finally crumbled. Overwhelmed by input, he had turned from passive receptor to active transmitter. His skin radiated the surplus he could no longer contain, pixels pulsing from every pore. It was his fate that finally decided me.

Barriers had burst, and everything was open. We were exposed, not just to the general flux, but to the thoughts and feelings of those close to us, and so I learned of Garcia's belief in me when we'd been together in the army, and I realised too what he had meant to me. I tried to help him through that last battle – but he was fighting the whole planet.

The world's thrashed systems needed a home for the information overspill. What more fitting home than the beings who had created the surfeit in the first place?

In that city, the authorities did their best to protect us, but the drifting meme-spore slipped invisibly through the interstices of the suits they'd equipped us with. Although the suits were faulty, we were ordered to wear them. It felt wrong to move round my home city like one of the old apollomen.

And so I departed – I could no longer endure the restrictions on my daily life, the clothes I wore and the places I went. I looked back, once, as I walked away. The sunlight was slanting low, and I could see the silver meme-cloud hanging bright over the suburbs.

So I came to this city, the city I'd been told was one long poem. As I approached, the sky above was clear. I stared curiously at the citizens as I trudged through the outskirts. None was wearing a suit.

I took a room in a cheap area, and began to find my way around. I appraised the people. No one was a transmitter, displaying message. I remembered Garcia, his torso alight with scrambled LCD that fragmented as his metabolism collapsed – *H lp m . Ple s .* But the flux I picked up here! In that first city I'd become panicked. I'd wanted out because I thought being a receptor was the inevitable prelude to death. Yet now – I embraced the receptor condition. I invited, I welcomed this new input, an emotive swell that suffused me in a warmth of wellbeing: *Bring all heaven before mine eyes ... Dissolve me into ecstasies...*

And there was even more by way of welcome. It was so easy to fall, what with all the passion in the air. In a food-store one day, my eyes met Anitra's... *So absolute she seems and in herself complete.* She held my gaze, and the poetry of her hit me viscerally, syllables of her music (*She fair, divinely fair, fit love for gods...*) thrilling along my veins, and I was captive.

Long hair, long skirts, dangling sleeves and jangling beads and bracelets. She was an artist, of course, and even wore flowers in her auburn hair. Big dark eyes that drew me in. "I love you," she said. Except she didn't say it. *Such sweet compulsion*, my heart rang, *such divine enchanting ravishment!*

City of poems and city of love! Slow mornings wandering the bazaar or laughing at Anitra assembling her crazy installations; the lazy lunches on a terrace overlooking the sea; afternoons wandering the sandy paths in the hills behind the city; the evenings on the beach watching the sun set over the ocean; and then the long nights, suffused in Anitra's ardour: *What hath night to do with sleep...?*

The exigencies of love had overwhelmed me and, if there was a silver haze appearing in the sky, I was the last to notice. I was in a new place and all my awareness went to reciprocating Anitra's passion. *Human face divine*, I sent her. *The loose train of thy amber-dropping hair...*

I felt enlivened, recharged, even as Anitra's rain of message became a torrent. Sleep gave no respite. Her message continued flooding me (*She all night long her amorous descant sang*) and I did my best to keep up, not knowing I wasn't in command of what I was doing. Anitra was drowning me in output, and all I could do was gush in return. It became a whole-body retch that I couldn't counter.

Then, the inevitable morning when I awoke, tattooed by livid meme.

"Anitra, we've got to stop this—"

That bewildering smile.

"Never," she said. "I have to message you. I have to. I'm not controlling this, you know. And neither are you. Look!"

She showed me her inner arm: *Both when we wake and when we sleep*

I tried to keep patient.

"You don't understand. Once message infiltrates your bones you start transmitting. Even decon won't save you then. I'm not messing here – we've got to stop!"

"How can we stop? You really love me, you know. You cover me in a coat of message! My leg, here, see... *With thee conversing I forget all time...*"

I gazed at the ardent glow that pulsed in my own flesh: *Heaven's last best gift, my ever new delight* ... I helplessly desired Anitra and my need shone gemstone-bright on the velvet of her skin: *Emparadised in one another's arms...*

We argued. Accusations and recriminations, raised voices and misunderstandings... Which always dissolved in Anitra's liquid laugh, my insistence melting, and our bodies falling together. Every time, her skin broadcast my craving and betrayed me. My longing for her was greater than my fear.

Today I stare at Anitra as we face each other, pores sparkling across both our naked bodies. She is luminescent, like a heavenly messenger.

"Anitra, please..."

My chest begins to glitter: *They hand in hand...*

I cannot help pulsing back pixels that glimmer on Anitra's torso: ... *With wandering steps and slow.*

We clasp and Anitra presses herself into me, whispering her love. She steps back. My chest and her breast both gleam with fervid verses.

"It doesn't have to be your way," says Anitra. "We should go in deeper, enfold it. What we have between us can beat it. And if we do go down, we go down together, shining."

Bodies entwined, we begin a new line.

The world was all before them...

Chris Bailey lives in Sheffield, UK, where he works as a college administrator. He reads a lot of poetry but feels he does not write it well so the lines quoted in the story come from someone who could, John Milton. Chris maintains that *Paradise Lost* is the first great SF narrative; his own, somewhat humbler, fictions have appeared in *Andromeda Spaceways* and others.

Junk Medicine

Die Booth

Art: Mark Toner

Donny can't make out what it is the kid's got, until she realises it's bitumen. This kid, she's almost certainly older than she looks, her baggy shirt nothing-coloured, made cheap without synthetic dyes. She's sitting on the kerb and gnawing on a little black lump of tar, as if that'll ease her symptoms any. It's been a while since Donny's even seen tar; she's surprised the girl managed to get hold of some. When the symptoms started getting acute, rumours spread that it would do as well as plastic and people started to smash up the old roads with picks and spades. The government told them it was pointless, like – you might as well hug a hot brick to cure pneumonia – but desperate people will believe anything that gives them hope.

"Hey–" Donny gives a little whistle between her two front teeth, "–you." The girl looks up, her guilty expression almost funny. Donny says, "You shouldn't be ruining your teeth on that crap. Get to a hospital." She could be fourteen, fifteen. Donny can't really tell. She squints against the corona sunlight, one hand shielding her eyes.

"You want a hand with your drums, mate?" Her voice is like a little boy voice, fluting but with a cracking edge.

Donny shakes her head. "We don't take on casuals," she says. The soles of her boots skid on the damp cobbles as she pushes the little hand cart that holds the oil drums up the restaurant service ramp. Pausing for breath at the top of the ramp, Donny's hand goes unconsciously to the front pocket of her work pants. The kid lifts one shoulder in a shrug. Donny can feel the girl watching right up until the service door bangs closed behind her.

"Filtration," says Donny, flicking her Kitts Biodiesel pass on its lanyard in the general direction of the kitchen overseer. The guy grunts and nods and doesn't look up from the magazine he's reading. The bald patch in the centre of his head is shiny with sweat. Donny sneers at him as she trundles past; she could be anyone, she could be brandishing a gun ready to steal the day's takings and he'd be none the wiser. Idiot is lucky to even have a job and he'll be luckier to keep it, acting that way. She glances down at her swinging work pass. *Senior filtration operative*. Glorified oil changer. The four little tin stars wink back the dim fluorescents: one star for each year she's been at Kitts; saving, saving... The trolley wheels squeak on the steam-wet floor and Donny pauses, trying to breathe; pushes a hand through her cropped hair sticking up stiff with the sweat that runs into her eyes. It's hot as arse in the kitchens, it always is. Too hot to wear her mandatory goggles without them steaming up. No business bothers with air con, the energy prices being the way they are, even though every summer seems to get closer and stiller and greyer.

The fryer's a hulking great 150 pound five-tuber, an old stainless steel one converted from gas to electric, squatting in the corner of the room under an extractor fan caked motionless with grime-blacked cobweb. At least they've let it cool, the surface of the oil frosted with scum. "Ugh... 'sake." Donny retrieves a submerged wire basket and dumps it onto the worktop, wiping congealing grease off her gloves onto her apron. It's barely worth using up a test strip – the oil's way past discard point, as even an uneducated glance would tell – but when she dips it anyway it turns predictably green. She leans against the worktop and lets her mind drift as the drainage pipe vomits sloppy chunks of sediment into the waiting drum. Daydreams a jigsaw of details: Asha. *The dimples at the base of her spine, the broad curves of her thighs, the fine dark line of hair across her upper lip. Her skin is perfect, glowing, smooth. She's spring breeze, she's cold beer, she's the tinkle of wind-chimes and the smell of hot tar on a summer-rainy night, she's...* The brass drainage line shudders and spits a last feeble gob of dirty yellow. Inside the tub the steel is stained a toxic orange, crusted burnt around the edges, and exuding the kind of over-cooked, weighty smell that clings in your sinuses. Donny expels a long breath. Pats her trouser pocket. She twists on the hot tap to run the first rinse bucket then picks up the long handled bristle brush from the trolley.

"All done here." The guy still doesn't trouble her with so much as a glance and Donny's double glad she cut corners with the job. So what if she boiled the cleaning agent for five minutes instead of twenty, and skipped the stabiliser? On the desk next to his propped up feet is a stack of paper napkins printed with the restaurant logo. *Carboneri's*. The more times she's called in to change their oil, the more money Kitts makes. Not that she'll be seeing this place in the next four years, judging by the state of what she's just sealed up in the drums on the trolley. Outside, slamming the van doors, she catches movement with the tail of her eye. A darker patch of murk in the shadows of the building: that kid still hanging around. Donny's hand hovers on the door, thumbnail tracing the rubber edge of the seal round the window. She's made up time cutting corners on this one. Next job's in thirty across town and she won't be losing any sleep if she's thirty late. She's got enough time to get back in the van and drive around for a while, throw this spy off her trail. But – she looks at the little figure, almost invisible, like a city mouse camouflaged on a railway track – the girl is just a child. Donny checks the doors are locked. She gives the shadowed shape a quick thumbs-up, wedges her hands into her stuffed pockets and sets off towards the street.

It's still muggy, but with a hanging mist of rain like the white sky is whinging. Maybe the relentless weather is what gives Donny that nape-crawling, storm-static nervousness, or maybe the feeling is understandable. It's quiet; the damp flags muffle her boots. The streets are typically empty and all she hears is a far-away hum of traffic and the distant whump-whump of roof turbines catching a rare, lofty wind. At a clipped echo behind, like a heel catching against a kerb, Donny turns sharply, but there's nobody there. She pretends to turn back, keeping a sly eye trained, and there she is: the girl. Donny chews on a smile, of relief as much as amusement. She could call her out, send her packing, but it'd probably only attract more attention and she's getting pushed for time and really, what harm can a kid do? Jogging across the road, she slips down a final side street, trailed by her new shadow, into the net of alleyways that runs between the high rises like cracks through rock.

She'd been expecting to wait a while, factored it in even, but the guy's already there when she arrives. He pushes off with one foot from the fence he's been lounging against, making the wire tower of it shudder all the way to the top, sending a couple of sparrows scolding into the air. A head shorter than Donny, his eyes scan, up and down the narrow pathway. When she reaches him, he sticks his hand out which is weird but she supposes nice. As they shake, he reaches into an inside pocket with the other hand and, passing her a small cardboard box, says, "This is it."

It feels surprisingly mundane when it's right there; like seeing a dead body. Except with this she can't quite divorce the money they're talking. "It's…"

"Yeah, ain't it? Beautiful."

She leaves it in the box, she just stares. She's seen photographs before, obviously, and cheap copies, but like her mum always said, you can't fake the real thing. It's a vivid, primary shade of green, clean and sleek, with three smooth beads moulded onto the band, like diamonds. "You sure it's plastic?" Donny's voice comes out a little more accusatory than she intended, but the guy doesn't seem put out in the slightest.

"Genuine PVC. None of your knock-off, corn-sugar Bakelite crap. Nineteen-eighties."

"Nineteen-eighties," Donny repeats.

"Woman I got it off had it valued a few years back at twenty K, but of course you know and I know it's not strictly legal to own it, so…" The guy purses his lips. "I mean, not like I ain't got a whole queue of buyers even so, but you're first on my list, so – let's just say, you're getting a bargain. OK?"

He doesn't try to look away when she makes proper eye contact with him. His eyes are really dark, barely showing the pupil,

which makes her think of Asha. And if he's fidgeting too much, static-pacing from one foot to the other, then it's not like anyone ever looks trustworthy anyway, not really. "OK," she says. The roll of notes sticks against her damp palm as she hands it over, shoving the ring box into her pocket.

"Nice doing business with you. Keep your contact on file?"

"Cheers. Don't bother," says Donny.

All in all, things are the worst they can be.

She's had that insistent feeling of being tailed from the moment she leaves the alleyway, then she notices the kid and hurries on. The feeling persists, though, the ring-box digging against her thigh. When she spots them, the first thing that occurs to her is to duck into the nearest open doorway, the kid slipping through behind her before the door closes. "You have to call the police." Donny hisses. The girl stares at her, vacant. She leans down a little, whispering urgently. "Call the – listen, call the police." A drop of cold sweat detaches itself from her nape and rolls down between her shoulder blades. If the police come and find her in possession of her beautiful contraband, it'll be confiscated and she'll be fined, but if the group of figures currently hanging around outside the front door of the shop… the door-bell on the end of its coiled brass spring dings merrily.

Donny swallows, closes her eyes briefly. "I'm not joking, kid, please, get the phone. You have to help me!"

"I'm not calling the police for you," says the girl in her flat, broad accent. Rising panic flares like acid in Donny's guts. "Where do you think he is, right now?" the girl says. Still staring, blankly, at – wait, not *at* Donny. Over her shoulder. At something – someone – over her shoulder.

"Oh." The seconds stretch. She makes herself turn. The figure's face is covered, even in this heat, except for the eyes. Donny's scalp seethes, her jaw tightens

"Fuck off, you," says the stranger. A man's voice. He cuffs the girl on the shoulder with the heel of his hand and she's off, sprinting like a hare at a shot. The guy turns back; Donny's blood rushes a silent scream. "We can do this hard, or we can do this easy."

His voice is low enough not to be overheard, measured enough to mimic normal conversation. Behind them, the shop keeper shuffles around, arranging magazines on a shelf above the counter. No need to involve him – the stranger's accomplices press masked faces against the windows – this is going to happen anyway. "Let's go outside," Donny says.

She thinks about running, but only for a heartbeat. There're four of them and they're dressed to not be recognised. "Give it here." A woman's voice: slight extra-terra accent; out of this world. It makes Donny remember with piercing clarity why she's doing this, why this failure is going to sting so much.

"You working with Hame?"

"Is that your fence? No. He didn't sell you out."

"That damn kid…"

The big guy laughs, booming like a sail in wind. "That skip-rat in the shop? Fuck off, we don't hire underage. We just know stuff. We watch. You weren't careful." His hand curls around Donny's collar.

As she hands the box over it strikes her as really funny that this situation has grown up around something so small. The box is tiny, not even palm-sized, and the big guy grabs it greedily, fumbling in the leather gloves that must be poaching him in his own sweat. A short laugh forces itself up from her guts, like a bubble through tar, just as he gets the lid off and lays eyes on the empty interior. Donny's ears sing as the masked woman lands her a crack around the temple. "*Where is it?*"

"It's gone?" It's awful, really, because she can't stop laughing, even when the other two start gouging fists into her belly and the big guy is shouting at her face so hard that his eyes above his bandana mask bug out white all around their blue irises. "Gone?" she keeps saying. It's all she can think of, the wobbly lines of bright pain behind her eyes like flat-lining life support, the whine of tinnitus mixing with the wail of an alarm and squealing brakes and then blue is added to the kaleidoscope of lights in her head and far away people are calling, "Shit. She ain't lying. It's gone. That kid. Run. Filth! Run!"

The trolley wheels squeak, sticking, and Donny gives one side a solid kick, the reverberation clanging through the empty metal drums. She leans forward, all her weight against the cart, to force it up the ramp. The front rail of it crashes into the *Carbonari's* logo painted in dirty, curly white on the black rear doors, but instead of pushing them open, it clangs to a bone-juddering halt. Donny groans, feeling it all the way up her arms. Jamming a foot against the wheels so it doesn't roll backwards, she pulls up one sleeve, inspecting her fading bruises. Some load of nothing to show for four years' savings. Then there's a screech of metal and she pitches forward as the doors are opened from the other side, and the balding security guard raises disinterested brows and waves her in. She follows his waddling shadow down the corridor towards the kitchens. Back already – some health inspector thing that placed blame on their hygiene more than Kitts's cleaning; whispered rumours of a rat in the fryer, closed until further inspection – this month has been full of surprises. If only some of them had been good. Even so, Donny boils the cleaning agent for a full half hour. She stirs in a textbook amount of stabiliser.

The sun's falling down in bloody pink bandages of cloud by the time she eases the full cart back down the service ramp, and: "Need any help with your drums, mate?"

She can't even muster the emotion to be angry. Rolling to a halt, she wipes her forehead with the back of one forearm and says, "Bit heavy for you when they're full."

The kid sidles out from behind the Kitts van. With the failing light casting big campfire shadows under her heavy brows and hollow cheeks she looks even rougher than before. She's wearing the same baggy track pants, her hands in the pockets, and when she pulls them out, something gleams neon between finger and thumb. "I only wanted a look at it." Donny reaches out, and she drops the ring into her open hand. "I thought I might swallow it, but it's too pretty." It is. It's too pretty. Donny stares at it, and then she stares at the kid with twin sunsets in her eyes. The girl frowns, then grins. "Who you giving it to?"

"Who says I'm giving it someone?" The kid tilts her chin up, sticks out her bottom jaw, hands back deep in her pockets. Donny nods, slowly. "Her name's Asha."

"You must love her loads." Another nod. "You gonna ask her to marry you?"

"Yeah," says Donny, but her voice comes out small and strangled like she's newly faced with a full-frontal of what all of this is for.

The kid sniffs. "Hope green's her colour."

"Every colour's her colour." Donny looks up, at every colour smeared across the sky, like a grease rainbow across a vat of oil. She tries to arrange her face to look stern at the girl, but it won't go into place, just keeps pinging back into a daft smile fit to reopen her split lip. The girl does a little skip on the spot, and looks over at the car park exit.

"You gonna ask her now? Tonight?"

Donny's heart drops the bass. "Yeah."

"You got to tell me what she says."

"If I see you. I don't come to this town much."

The girl smiles with one side of her mouth. She rubs her nose with the back of her hand. "I'm around."

Donny can't think of anything to say, so she just nods again. The kid glances at the exit gate once more like she's dying to make a run for it and for some reason Donny feels the same. "I got to go, yeah."

"Yeah." The girl makes a vague gesture with one hand that might be a thumbs-up. Halfway across the car park she looks back over her shoulder and calls, "She's gonna say yes."

"I know." Donny says, probably too quiet for the kid to hear. She watches until the little figure is absorbed back into the tarry black city shadows, then she unlocks the rear doors of the van and starts hefting the full drums into the back. Night's drawing in and for once there's the slightest whisper of breeze. It could be her imagination, but she could swear that from somewhere she can hear the faint song of wind chimes.

Die Booth lives in Chester and enjoys exploring dark places. His short story collection *My Glass is Runn* and *365 Lies* – one flash fiction a day for a year, with profits going to the MNDA – are out now.
http://diebooth.wordpress.com/ @diebooth

As part of the **Visual Words** series, we are proud to present Luna's first Comic: **Apollo Unbound**. Written by **Chris Kelso**. Illustrated by **Jim Agpalza**.

Hollywood icon Apollo Calloway has woken up in the unlikeliest of places - rural Ayrshire. A leader of the estate or a scapegoat of fate, Apollo prepares for his ultimate performance...

"Someday soon people are going to be naming him as one of their own influences. He's worth checking out."– INTERZONE magazine

"Jim Agpalza's art is 100% pure concentrated aggro. Disturbingly terrific." - Seb Doubinsky, author of The Babylonian Trilogy

Release date 18/11/2017

Science Fiction, Fantasy & Dark Fantasy in Fiction and Academia.

Scottish Independent Press.

Est. 2015

As part of the **Visual Words** series, we are proud to present our new illustrated novellette:

Final Diagnosis.
Written by **Peter Garrett**.
Illustrated by **Simon Walpole**.

In the port city of Searcy, murder is no longer a common occurrence, despite its history of violence. But when a senior psychiatrist is found with his head quite literally emptied out, it seems things might be about to take a dark turn. For DI Shaymie Sjaemusson, it marks the beginning of an investigation unlike any before, even as he's forced to confront a deep trauma from his childhood.

As if things couldn't get any stranger, all evidence points to a perpetrator that may not be human. And then, a myth from the dawn of human sentience appears from the shadows.

Release date 30/11/2017

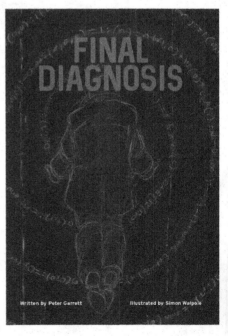

ATU334 the Wise

Marija Smits

Runner-up
Shoreline of Infinity Flash Fiction
Competition 2017

Art: Becca McCall

Baba Yaga was not one for reminiscing, but she'd had a difficult day, a dull day, and wanted nothing more than to sit by her starry fireplace with a cup of chamomile tea and to remember the good old days. The days when her house used to dance and twirl on its chicken legs, the days when she used to fly about in a mortar, her broom sweeping the skies. Those were the days when she had the power to amaze and frighten people. But now that they had their own spaceships, as well as the physical and mental enhancements that made them so much more, and so much less, they were no longer so in awe of her.

Still, she consoled herself, her new home wasn't so bad. It had some fine views of the universe, a few plants at the windows, and a black hole not too far away. It was comforting to be so close to something so dangerous, so like herself, and its accretion disk was spectacular.

My! But what an age it had been since that Russian girl, Vasilisa, so innocent, and yet so wise, had come to visit her. Baba Yaga sighed and then chuckled as she recalled a more recent visitor. Humanity was still able to throw her the odd interesting challenge. This girl – or was she more AI than girl? – had come to her house, asking for light. And this girl, unlike so many, had actually seemed wary of her.

Baba Yaga, out of habit, had agreed to give her the light, but only if she was successful in carrying out the three tasks she set for her. If the girl (who called herself ATU334) failed to complete the challenges she'd be killed. Exterminated. Vaporized. Squished. Of course they were impossible challenges, way beyond the girl's computational abilities, and Baba Yaga had begun to relish the idea of sending the girl to her death.

But the girl had surprised her by completing the tasks.

How did you do it? Baba Yaga had asked.

The girl had tapped her head. *By my mother's blessing.*

Baba Yaga had grimaced. *What blessing?*

An instinct chip that my mother had gifted me with on her death.

Baba Yaga scowled; she gave the girl the starlight from her fireplace and sent her packing.

Later, Baba Yaga had made enquiries of the girl. Apparently, she'd taken the starlight back home to her cruel clone sisters – the ones who'd sent her out on the dangerous errand in the first place – and then the starlight had incinerated them. The girl, wise enough not to mess with a growing star, had thrown it up into the heavens, where it quickly drew a system of planets towards it.

Baba Yaga sighed, sipped a little more tea. She shook her head, muttered, 'Instinct chips. Whatever next?'

Right on cue, there was a knock at the door.

Baba Yaga grinned.

Marija Smits is the pen-name of Dr Teika Bellamy, a mother-of-two, ex-scientist and editor whose art and writing has appeared in a variety of publications. When she's not busy with her children she's running the indie press, Mother's Milk Books. 'Teika' means 'fairy tale story' in Latvian.

If Thine Eyes

Offend Thee

Daniel Rosen

Art: Becca McCall

In my younger and more vulnerable years, Mother often asked me what I wanted to be when I grew up. The answer was always the same. I wanted to be a mermaid. Not a princess, or a programmer, or a performance analyst, but a perfect creature of the sea.

That just encouraged Mother. When she was a girl, she wanted to be a princess, and she'd grown up to become Miss Oregon. She was living proof that with the right combination of hard work, rigorous discipline, and artful body reconstruction, you could bring your dreams to life. I was lucky. Mother supported my dreams from an early age: she got me my first cosmetics playset when I was four, my first breast implants when I was fourteen. "You can become anything in the world, Elsa." she'd say, smiling warmly. I became a model. Back then, the only operations you needed were a couple strategically placed synthetic plastic sacs. You didn't need to devote yourself to your art like we do today. Back then, a supermodel could still be human.

If I'd known what it entailed, I wouldn't have gotten the fins. I don't think so, anyway. But I didn't know. And besides, I liked my life. It might have had its ups and downs, but at the end of the day, modelling really let me express myself. You become what you pretend to be, you know, and by that metric I'd always been a mermaid. I just didn't realize at first that I needed to be the best.

So when the Voice gave me the green light, I'd already slipped into the water. My scaled breasts and seaweed hair floated lazily in the low gravity grotto pool. The whirring of shutters filled the air around me as photo drones dove down to catch all my angles. I spun once, twice, rolling over onto my side and just coasting through the water, motionless.

"That's perfect, Elsa. Can you arch your back for us? Like you just woke up. Kitten in the sun stuff." The Voice came from all the drones simultaneously, a perfect buzzing harmony. You never knew if it was a person or program giving cues, but it didn't matter. The Voice knew how to work an audience.

I arched my back.

"Perfect."

I could almost hear the applause. It was easy to imagine my image being projected out to billions of consoles, the lapping of my watery grotto filling homes all across the world. The viewers were my family. My mothers and fathers. My lovers. My fans.

That was my life. Some blissful three hours later, after the clicking shutters had slowed and the gravity slowly came back, life sank back in. My bills, my diet, my exercise program. The loans for all my colored scales. They weighed heavier and heavier, out of the water. It was harder to manoeuvre in and of out of my wheelchair sometimes, even when I had support staff to help. Thoughts like these came and went like tides when I was out of water.

The call came after a particularly long and gruelling night of shooting. The support staff had already gone home, so I shifted my bulk into the back seat on my own while the console rang insistently.

"Elsa Berhault?"

"That's me."

The voice on the other side cleared its throat. It was gravelly, but high-pitched, the sound of scree rattling on a steep street. "Good evening, Elsa. I represent Cosmos Unlimited. Sorry to bother you so late, is now a good time to talk?"

Cosmos Unlimited. The cherry at the top of the Big Five international beauty pageants. The big leagues. To my credit, I stayed calm. I'd been waiting on this call for a long time.

"I'm free for at least a half-hour." *Breathe.*

"First of all, congratulations. We saw your performance tonight, and frankly, we were blown away. How would you feel about competing in this year's Miss Cosmos competition?"

I said nothing about how desperately I wanted it. I didn't tell the gravelly voice how many years I'd applied to be considered as a Miss Cosmos contestant. I didn't tell him that, in fact, I applied this year and they rejected me. That's not how this business works.

Instead, I said: "That sounds like something I could be interested in. I'll have my agent iron out the details with you, but why don't you tell me about it?"

I spent the rest of the car ride half-awake, letting the high-pitched rasp lull me into a dreamlike state with stories of past competitors, prize money, and oceans of everlasting glory and fame.

When I got home, I packed my bags with the bare essentials. All my cosmetics, my moisturizers and pH balancers. Scales in every spectrum of the rainbow, and a few beyond, in case we shot in the dark, or ultraviolet. My sac of pterois venom. A small can of mace. Weapons, all of them.

The Miss Cosmos competition was not a place for soft creatures.

Twelve hours later, I was in Dubai, sitting in a hotel tub and sipping Tanqueray. Even a single glass had too many calories, but I felt like celebrating.

I only had one night before shooting started — they put me in as a late registrant, not unheard of. Mermaids have been a hot ticket over the past few months, beating out fairy wings and cat ears by a huge margin in focus groups. Thing was, Cosmos already had a mermaid. *The* mermaid. My competition.

Marie Lavielle: 34C cups, 24 inch waistline, 35 inch hips. 6'4" with the elegantly feathered tail of a lionfish. She's the reigning champion of Miss Cosmos, the reason it's so hard for other fins to get in. Fortunately, I had a plan to deal with her.

As I heaved myself up and out of the tub, I wondered if Marie was staying in the same hotel, the Imperial. She might be taking a bath right now too, smoothing and polishing her scales. though I guessed she didn't indulge in gin. I pulled myself into a waiting wheelchair and slid into a dry bathrobe, then rolled out into the hallway. There was a vending machine just a few doors down, and I needed gum to take the piney taste of Tanqueray out of my mouth.

There was a bushy tailed fox girl leaning against the wall under recessed LED lights, skin as smooth as eggshell, hair as black as night. She was pulling on a vaporizer and blowing out fat rings of hazy blue.

"I saw your grotto stuff yesterday. Pretty good."

I nodded. "Thanks. I'm Elsa."

"Victoria." She pulled again and offered me the vaporizer. "You want a drag of this? Only 15 milligrams."

"Sure." I puffed away, unable to conjure up the rings that Victoria the fox girl had so effortlessly spat about. The vapor tasted like blueberries.

"You're new this year, right?"

"I don't know that I'd say I'm new. This is my first year in Miss Cosmos, but I've been modelling for a long time." I gestured expansively up and down the length of my mostly scaled body, from hair to fins.

"Well, word to the wise." She took her vaporizer back and sucked at it. "Don't talk with anybody else. There's a lot of backstabbing, and some weird shit goes down behind the scenes. You just can't trust anyone, you know?"

I grinned. "Does that include you?"

She didn't smile back. "What do you think?"

I bought a pack of Blizzard Blast and rolled back to my room. We had our first shoot in the morning, and I wanted to be sure I got plenty of sleep. I was already tired, and I only just made it into the bathtub before I lost consciousness.

I woke up to the ringing of my console, mouth dry, eyes crusted with gunk. The clock read 10:20. I'd slept for almost twelve hours.

This meant I was quite unfashionably late.

I rolled out of the tub and raced down the hallway as quickly as I could, wheels whirring as I picked up speed on the carpeted straightaways. A short blonde assistant was already waiting in the lobby when the elevator doors opened, and her expression was mixed frustration and relief when she saw me.

"Elsa?"

I nodded.

"You're in deep shit. You were supposed to show up for make-up at 9am."

I shrugged, and she muttered something unintelligible under her breath.

"Maybe we should get going?" I said. She rolled her eyes and wheeled me out to a waiting limo.

The photo shoot was in the Keep of the Four Elements, on one of the terraformed islands just off the coast. I'd never actually been inside a Dubai arcology. The Keep was a huge Gothic structure made of quartz-veined granite and thick glass sheets, complete with old-fashioned flying buttresses. Inside, they boasted jungles and beaches and deserts and marshes and mountains and snowy pine forests. Here, I saw what humans had achieved as a species, effortlessly quilting together any environment they pleased. It made me ache for legs again, to experience all of these different places with my feet and hands and heaving lungs.

The assistant, who'd told me to call her YT, just pushed my chair from one environment to another without a care in the world. She didn't seem even the tiniest bit impressed.

"Never been in an arcology, huh?" she said as I gaped out at a herd of gazelles.

"No." One of the gazelles looked up at us, then returned to its grazing, unconcerned with our presence. "How do you get used to all of this?" I waved my arms around me.

"I was born here."

"Must be nice."

She didn't say anything, and soon we reached a small building nestled at the crux of all the environments, an axle at the center of this gargantuan quilted wheel. The heart of the Keep of the Four Elements.

Inside, the seeming placidity of the arcology was shattered. People wearing headsets and unusual body modifications stalked around with menacing purpose, photo drones zipping around above them like a hive of disturbed wasps. The walls of the building were covered floor-to-ceiling in consoles.

Before I knew it, one of the headset stalkers had grabbed my chair and wheeled me to one side, dusting me with mica and swabbing me with glittering gel.

"Sorry I'm late. I slept in."

The make-up artist said nothing, squeezing and smoothing me. Then for the first time that morning, I thought about Victoria. What had she been doing sitting around the vending machine? Was it really just nicotine that I'd smoked, or something more sinister?

"You're on in five. They're shooting you in the desert today." Then the make-up artist took a step back and squinted at me. "You'd better hurry."

Five minutes later, I was wheeled out into the desert, disoriented and dizzied by the sudden rush of heat. I had no experience shooting in places like this, hot and dry and harsh and sandy. Marie was sitting in her own wheelchair, a floating suspensor model, smiling at me. It was a cruel smile, the smile of a shark or a barracuda just before it strikes.

The drones whirred around me, and then suddenly, without warning, the commands came.

"Try opening up your eyes a bit more, Elsa, we really need to see those peepers."

I tried to widen my eyes, doing my best not to cry whilst being whipped by hot sand.

"Really open them up! We're not here to see you look like an unearthed cave creature, right?"

That's when the tears came.

47

The shoot went poorly, to say the least. I was out of my element, and every time I got a cue, I messed it up. Still, it must have been worse for some of the others. Even though half the contestants are cut every round, there were still four left. I was one. So was Marie Lavielle. I caught Marie staring at me during the ceremony, sucking on her lower lip.

Then came the announcement. I was out. It was close, with me getting cut off right after Victoria. I saw the fox girl right at the end, when they made the announcement. She shrugged and waited for me, then began to wheel me away. Maybe she meant to be friendly, but I wanted to kill her. I wanted to break her and roll over her again and again in my chair, until her bones had been rendered into wet dust. I let her wheel me all the way back to my room and offered me another drag of her vaporizer. I rolled my eyes, and she smiled.

"Fool me once, huh?"

"I'm sorry you didn't make the cut." She said, lying through her pointed teeth. She wasn't sorry at all. It was my own fault for letting her dose me. I needed to be more careful. Miss Cosmos was not a place for soft creatures.

"Yeah, well, next year, right?" She took a long drag, exhaled the sweet smell of once-chewed bubblegum and cotton candy. "You know, you're not so bad, Elsa."

"That's what I keep telling myself." Then I had an idea. "I'd be doing even better if I could get a good night's sleep. I can't seem to get my bathtub working."

She wrinkled her nose. "There shouldn't be any non-contestants staying here."

I shrugged.

Victoria took another drag, thinking. "You could just take my room."

"Why would you do that? Why should I trust you?"

Cue vicious laugh. "Elsa, you're out. Done. You'll have to wait until next year. Besides, I feel bad for slipping you opiates yesterday. I owe you."

"You're a wretched creature." *And I'll pay back your debt.*

"I prefer 'vixen'." She winked. "All's fair in love and war, right?" My mind raced. "Ok," I say. "Let's switch rooms. Just let me get back and pack up my things first."

A minute later, I'd rolled back to my room and packed everything away, with the exception of my pterois venom, which I sprinkled liberally into all the tea and coffee in the room. Then I took a bar from my wheelchair and bent the faucet of the bathtub. I was briefly thankful for the strength I'd gained by being wheelchair-bound. I rolled around and stared critically at my room. Yes. It was perfect. An eye for an eye. Now I just needed to make sure I was on camera all night and I'd be fine.

I got up early before the second day of shooting, but there was no sign of Victoria down by the vending machine. A knock on the door of my old room yielded no response. I hoped she enjoyed sleeping in.

YT was waiting for me in the lobby.

"Were you here this time yesterday?" I said.

"Of course."

"So you could have come up to my room and woken me up. Pounded on the door or something."

"It's not my responsibility to babysit contestants. I just make sure you can get to and from the photo shoots."

As YT helped me into the car, I admired the strength in her core, the versatility of her smooth arms and legs. She was graceful, even crumpling a mermaid girl into the backseat.

"Have you ever thought about getting any operations, YT?"

"No."

"Not that you need one. You look great already. But you've never even thought about it?"

YT said nothing until goodbye, after she wheeled me into the heart of the Keep and left me there in a small room with the remaining three contestants. They were legends, the lot of them. There was Synthelle, the glittering white plastic girl, who started life as a double amputee. Old now, at 106. As old as Mother had been when she died. Then Aurora, blue and chitinous, who opted to undergo the first full exoskeletal surgery. Her eyes glittered compound red, sparkling light into every corner of the little room.

Then the mermaids: Marie Lavielle and me. Marie sat in her suspensor chair, a fancy model that kept her raised up high off the floor. Her fins were elegantly feathered, floating through the air around her as if by magic. I reminded myself that she was not a goddess. More than human, perhaps, but not perfect.

The ever-present drones swarmed over our heads, and we all did our best not to stare at each other. The others did a better job.

"We've cancelled today's photoshoot," the Voice said.

I glanced sidelong at the others. Auroras antennae flickered faintly, but the other two didn't react at all. They were seasoned veterans. Perhaps they know something I don't, but I've never heard of a shoot being cancelled during the Miss Cosmos competition before. Disappearances, deaths, sure. But cancelling the shoot?

"Victoria Tamamo-no-Mae was found dead this morning." The Voice rang out in chorus from all the drones above. There was a long pause. "We'd prefer not to alert the authorities. Do any of you have anything to say for yourself? Any admission of guilt?"

Silence.

"The body was found in the room of Elsa Berhault." The uncomfortable silence grew worse, and I could feel the gazes of the other contestants fall on me. A drone dropped down and hovered in front of me.

"We traded rooms last night." I said, willing myself not to sweat. There was no way for them to know I'd killed Victoria. Besides, of the two mermaids here, there was only one with venomous glands. Marie Lavielle was toast. "My bathtub wasn't working properly, and she offered to trade with me." Then I played the rest of my hand. "I did a short private shoot last night, though. You can check the records, I was in my room all night." I kept my voice weak and shaky.

"And you didn't alert the hotel itself to any of this?"

"No." If only.

The drone spun and buzzed over to Marie. "Do you have an alibi for yesterday evening, Ms. Lavielle?"

"No."

"You might be interested in knowing that the body of the deceased carried traces of pterois venom. The same poison you have in your own implanted lionfish glands, according to your official body modification registry." The tension in the room grew, and I held down my smile when Marie looked over at me, eyes narrowed. "The competition resumes tomorrow, pending investigation. According to Cosmos rules, Elsa Berhault will take up the 4th place position in place of Victoria Tamamo-no-Mae."

The next day, news sources reported that famed kitsune supermodel Victoria Tamamo-no-Mae had been found dead in an apparent suicide. There was no mention of suspects, or murder. No surprise. There was a long history of contestants going missing, although it usually didn't end in murder. The Miss Cosmos contest had always been merciless. They cared about pulling money from viewers, not the welfare of the contestants. Besides, the laws in Dubai offered lot of leeway when it came to events out of the public eye.

The murder had clearly shaken Synthelle and Aurora, a silver lining. They were slow to respond to the Voice. They missed cues, took too long to hit their angles. At the end of the day, they didn't look good. If only it'd had some effect on Marie.

She didn't seem affected at all. She was a goddess that day. She moved in mysterious ways, finding her place before the Voice had even given a cue. She spun like a dervish. She was perfect. I loved and hated her.

It came down to the final day. I'd made it to the last round. Just two contestants left, two mermaids and suspected murderers. For the final shoot, they decided they'd put us in the same glistening watery grotto. The whole set was lit by phosphorescent jellyfish. The trick, it seemed, would be not to let the jellyfish foul up your fins as you turned and spun underwater.

I was first, having scored lower than Marie in the previous shoots. I sat at the edge of the grotto, half-immersed, letting my heart beat to the buzzing drones and lapping water around me.

"Ok, go ahead, Elsa." came the Voice.

Almost as soon as I dove in, I could tell that the jellyfish were going to be a problem. They kept catching at my dorsals, the long trailing fins at my hips. They were mostly decorative, and in that moment I cursed ever having gotten them.

"Don't muck up the lighting!" I came to a stop and worked myself free of the jellyfish. Every time I tried to move, however, I kept catching my fins on the damned invertebrates. "OK, Elsa, that's enough. Come on back."

I pulled myself up and out of the water, slipping once on the mossy stone. Marie smirked.

That was it. That was going to be how I lost the Miss Cosmos contest.

My heart dropped as she sank gracefully into the pool, her fins trailing out behind her in the halo of an aquatic angel. Then, miraculously, I was saved. Marie's huge feathery fins fared even worse than mine had. The jellyfish clustered around her like flies on rotten meat.

"No, no, no." said the Voice, frustrated. "Let's try Elsa again."

I dove back in eagerly, moving slowly and meticulously, avoiding each and every one of the cursed creatures. Still, just the drift of the current was enough for the jellies to catch at me and cling. The Voice called for Marie again, and I crawled out of the water.

Then, suddenly, watching Marie struggle with the jellyfish, I knew what I had to do. I needed one last change to my body. One last modification.

The grotto was carved of stone, and away from the pool, they'd left surfaces unfinished, jagged and sharp at the edges. I went deeper into the cave and found one spine of granite that looked particularly keen.

I sawed my hips against the spine, gritting my teeth against the pain as I rubbed my dorsal fins against it. I ground myself up and down against the stone until it was slick with blood and ragged flesh. I had both sides done when the Voice called my name again.

Marie came out of the water gasping, and it was my turn to smirk, pale-faced, as I lowered myself into the water. The water was salty, and it stung my open sides.

"Ok, Elsa, just try to swim across. Let's just try to get a shot here. This is going out to billions of people right now, right? Don't waste that."

I smiled and kicked, twirling as I cut through the water, weaving scarlet threads in my wake, wisps of crimson spreading out through the water. I was slick, and even when we came into contact, I slid right by the luminescent jellyfish. I no longer had any fins to interfere with the lighting. I was free. I was perfect for this shoot.

"That's perfect, Elsa. Now give us that arch. Bare yourself." The Voice rumbles like through the water in a sticky molasses bass.

I imagined Marie Lavielle, realizing her loss. She didn't have the drive. She didn't have the discipline required to get rid of unnecessary parts. I arched my back.

"Perfect."

In the Voice, I could hear the held breath of a captive audience. I imagined them pointing out each tendril of blood, and my sawed off fins. I realized in that moment that the suffering made us most beautiful. It was the hardships and fears and pain we endured that made our viewers love us. My audience wept with my pain, and laughed with my joy. They shared with me. I am a goddess, and the audience is my congregation. They are my devoted. My flock.

Someone out there is saying: "I know her."

They are saying: "I need her."

They are saying: "I love her."

Daniel Patrick Rosen writes speculative fiction by day and swing jazz by night. He grew up on a tiny farm in northern Minnesota, where he was nourished by raw venison steak and oversteeped Earl Grey. His work has appeared in *Apex*, *IGMS*, and *Lackington's*.
You can find him online at http://rosen659.wix.com/avantgardens and @animalfur on Twitter.

Pauline and the Bahnians

SK Farrell

Runner-up
Shoreline of Infinity Flash Fiction
Competition 2017

Dear Commander Jeffers,

I was surprised to receive your communication this morning: apologies for the delay in replying. I saw the machine merrily printing out spool, but then glanced outside and noticed that the chickens had escaped again. By the time I'd rounded up the Orpington, it was time for lunch.

You mentioned the neural transceiver. Now, the whole point of living Edgewards was peace and quiet, so I made David disconnect it when I moved in, I'm afraid. The alphasender is enough for me. You seem to have the hang of it, but don't be shy about varying your punctuation. All those stops are very military, but jolting to read.

Onto the main topic of your message: a Bahnian invasion? Bahnian's not a word I'm familiar with. Although, if you're talking about the flowering climbers taking over my strawberry patch, I'm all ears.

Best wishes,

Pauline.

Dear Commander,

You're right, the alphasender is dated technology. It does lowercase letters, though. I didn't know either, to begin with, but David – my grandson – explained it. Apparently my first messages home caused some hilarity.

I have eight grandchildren. I survived five wars, and had my brainstate copied and relayed Edgewards aged 89. I might not have a rank, but I consider longevity to be qualification enough, and I do not care for your tone.

Here I am, in my own home, bombarded with foul language and threats about protocols, defences, batteries and Bahnians (what IS a Bahnian, please?). I won't stand for it.

I've replied politely, and am due an explanation.

Respectfully,

Pauline.

Dear Commander,

Thanks for your reply. Apology accepted. No, those coordinates are correct. SY79BA16Z2P: my cottage. I definitely wouldn't have moved next to a military installation!

The Bahnians sound repulsive. I've always thought, though, that the races we've stumbled upon since our leap to the stars are creatures like us, and have an equal right to life. I'm a gardener, so am acquainted with the pain of slugs, but I don't commit gastropod genocide in the vegetable patch. Something to think about.

I'd have noticed laser cannons in my cottage, or aliens lurking behind the chicken coop. All's quiet here.

Regards,

Pauline.

Commander,

If you insist SY79BA16Z2P is an outpost, I'll fetch the estate agent's deeds from the attic.

Pauline.

Dear Commander,

I must admit, I've never looked through these in detail before. It WOULD appear that SY79BA16Z2P was a Federation outpost, but the certificates say it was decommissioned once the Edge was abandoned as an Area of Prime Development. Fascinating!

Yet in your last message, you were certain of its active status.

This concerns me. The estate agent seemed a decent chap, but they're not known for their honesty, are they? Have I been scammed? I've put a lot of work into this cottage. That chicken coop didn't build itself, and the shrubs are well-established now. I need a sit down.

Pauline.

Dear Commander,

A kind reply. Yes, legal faffing about can wait. We should focus on these Bahnians. There IS a particularly bright body in the sky: it's an attractive blue, and I thought it might be a new star, but now you mention it, maybe it does have a fuel trail.

I haven't changed my mind about the universe. Diplomacy is always best with alien governments.

What you wrote about the 'host body' and 'dissolving' and 'cranial probing', however, possibly rules these Bahnian fellows out.

David is away in the Riley System, so I can't ask him about fixing the transceiver. You, therefore, can't beam instructions in real time, but if you send a basic overview of how to operate the emplacement, I'm sure I can work it out. I've got a keen eye from my embroidery.

Pauline.

Dear Commander,

Instructions received.

Referring to the cottage blueprints, I located the laser battery and deployed the prime weapon. Unfortunately, it was under the henhouse, which smashed to pieces when the metal trapdoors burst open. No casualties: the Orpington was dazed, and the Dorking lost two tail feathers, but I scooped them up and sequestered them in the pantry. Chaos, but needs must.

Pauline.

Dear Commander,

Rousing words in your last message: very Henry V, if I may.

My report.

Just after dinner, I could see through the laser viewfinder that the blue body had turned towards my position. At that magnification, it was clearly a craft that matched your description: weird, incomprehensible protrusions and shimmering fields.

I tracked the ship, and pondered.

I thought about slugs, Commander.

But I also thought about my grandchildren, scattered through the galaxy, and my great-grandsons, growing up brave in colonies. I concluded that we must live and let live, but if something threatens to harm us for no good reason, we mustn't take that sort of thing lying down.

I pressed the button.

You didn't tell me how beautiful military laser fire is. The beams scorched through the sky, blazing strawberry neon bright, following some rhythmic pattern sent from the computer. Then the explosions. Magnificent! Minutes, they lasted, on and on as the fuel tanks caught and ever tinier pieces coruscated across the heavens.

I watched, though my eyes ached with afterimages. Nothing moved up there. Nothing at all.

We got those tentacular bastards, Commander, and gave any others something to think about.

If it's alright, I should very much like to sleep.

Pauline.

Dear Jeffers,

My gratitude for the mention of medals, but we don't go in for pomp in my family.

It's nice of you to offer to visit, too. It's a small place, especially when you consider the furniture, plants, artwork and animals I've accumulated. So while the kettle's always on, it would be best if you came alone. There isn't room for a fleet, and if you came on 'official business', so to speak, we might get into that legal nonsense about whose property this is, and neither of us would enjoy that.

The laser's still armed, by the way.

Much love,

Pauline.

SK Farrell writes SF and fantasy, and lives near Edinburgh. She is an English teacher and mother of serpents. Her short fiction can be read in the BFS's *Horizons #5*, and she is working on her first novel. She can be found pottering around the garden, or on Twitter @sk_farrell.

The Apple Bee

K.E. Macphee

Art: Stephen Pickering

There it was again: a muffled buzzing, coming from somewhere inside the station. Now that the noise had reached his conscious awareness, the man was unable to ignore it. He eased himself from his cross-legged sitting position. It had been some years since he'd been able to stretch his joints into a full lotus, and perhaps, some day soon, even sitting like this on a hard floor would be too much. He let out a long breath, loosening his shoulders with slow circular movements and shaking his legs to restore their circulation. His feet were tingling, just as they used to when he first began a daily meditation practice, so many years ago. "Full circle," he murmured to himself, then went to find the source of the buzzing.

As he'd suspected, the noise was coming from a bee. He found it spinning on the floor of the kitchenette area, just beneath the open window. His knees let out two loud pops as he crouched down to examine the insect. The bee had a badly damaged right wing, and was clearly unable to fly. Without rising from his squat, the man reached up for the drinking glass that was standing on the benchtop next to the sink, then laid it sideways on the floor. With a deft sweep of his fingers, he propelled the bee into the glass. He stood up again, holding the edge of the bench for balance, and put the glass back where he'd found it. First, some breakfast.

He found it amusing that he still used different words for different meals – breakfast, lunch, dinner. The food itself varied not at all: a relentless medley of potatoes, maize, barley and, of course, apples, plus the occasional ancient ration pack for nutritional balance. He sometimes thought wistfully of other plant foods – what he'd give for a last bean or berry! – but the variety was limited by practicality; the bees were apple bees, so apart from the apples, only self-pollinating crops would have lasted this long.

Apples! He looked out of the window towards the tracts of apple orchard sheltering in the semi-circular valley. When he'd started here, the orchard had been small and clinical. Over the years, by collecting pips, nurturing seedlings and developing fresh soil-beds, he'd extended its range tremendously, until he finally ran out of irrigation tubing for the solar distillers. Quite early on, he'd abandoned the neatly-organised rows and began planting saplings wherever he fancied, red by green by yellow, eaters next to cookers. The rambling orchard now produced more apples than he could ever hope to use: Macouns and McIntoshes, Cortlands and Criterions, Galas and Gravensteins. Some of these varieties were rare even when they were first planted; by now, they might be the only remaining examples of their kind. Sharp, sweet, white-fleshed, pink-fleshed, smooth-skinned or russet, he knew them all, by name, by growth habits and by taste.

He scraped some of the potatoes he'd cooked two days ago into a bowl, then ate them standing up at the bench. Lately, he'd been trying to cook less often and in larger quantities. It was more energy-efficient that way, and it meant he always had some edible food on hand. The cabin's solar array was still working well, but the storage batteries attached to it were now almost useless, having been charged and drained for many thousands of cycles beyond their intended lifespan. When the sun was shining strongly, he had full power, but at other times he had to use his electrical equipment sparingly, switching one thing off when he wanted to use another. He had no power at all at night, so he'd gotten into the habit of waking at dawn and returning to his bed as soon as the sun fell behind the mountainous ridges at the back of the valley.

He glanced at the potatoes remaining in the big pot, which looked no different than they had the day he'd cooked them. The absence of airborne yeasts and moulds and other microbes had turned out to be a blessing: although it meant that the soil needed laborious preparation and treatment before it could grow anything, it also allowed his produce, once harvested, to be stored for many seasons. Facing a growing surplus of apples, he'd started using them to make artworks, laying out huge mosaic apple-pictures down on the old transit pad. His first works had been simple geometric patterns, but as time went by and he grew more confident, he began making representational images: people, places, animals that he remembered. He'd leave each picture until it became over-familiar, and then he'd gather up the apples, stack them back into colour-sorted piles and begin anew. It was very satisfying, and the picture-work had become a highlight of his waking hours.

His current apple-picture was nearly finished, and he planned to work on it again today – but first there was the bee to deal with. He smiled. He'd grown irrationally fond of his bees, and now felt almost fatherly towards them. He needed them, and it made him happy when they occasionally needed him in return. He put down his empty bowl and picked up the drinking glass, in which the bee was still circling aimlessly. He held up the glass at eye level and inspected the bee from various angles. Apart from the damaged wing, it seemed to be in good condition. That was encouraging. He hated to lose even a single bee, although, inevitably, their numbers were lower now than they had been when he and the hive first arrived. There was some natural attrition, and there were no other hives on the island that might be used to boost his own bee population. The bees were just another limited resource, another challenge to get by with what he had, to make things last for as long as he could – for as long as he himself could last.

He'd been lucky, he knew that. No man would survive in good health for long on a diet of potatoes, maize and apples. The station had been equipped with a year's freeze-dried rations, but they wouldn't have kept him alive all these years. He was fortunate that some half-prescient militarocrat had concealed a storage facility on the far side of the island: half-prescient, because while it had clearly been correct to anticipate disaster, nonetheless whatever disaster had come was evidently so unexpected, or so overwhelming, that the stored materials were never accessed.

He'd found the bunker a few weeks after satellite communication with the main outpost had abruptly ceased. By then, his emotions had built up into a roiling tangle that no amount of daily meditation could calm: frustration at not knowing what had happened, fear that whatever nameless peril had befallen the outpost might also be heading towards his island, and a growing, panicky suspicion that the others had departed because of some greater calamity elsewhere, and had simply – and permanently – left him behind. In the end, not knowing what else to do, he packed up a hiking sack with several weeks' provisions, took the satellite radio and set off around the coastline. Perhaps he secretly hoped that the communication failure was due to some local vagary, that the satellite radio might burble back into life if he travelled far enough from the station – but how far could he travel, a man on a small island surrounded by an entire planetary hemisphere of ocean? He had no flyer, no boat. He knew he could go nowhere, in the end, except back where he started.

After three days of walking, he'd reached the far, wide end of the pear-shaped island. He was on the previously unseen side of the peaks that ringed the station's valley. Back there, near the station, the horse-shoe of peaks gently subsided into low hills running out to meet a flat, slender peninsula. At this end of the island, they were relentlessly jagged, with sheer cliffs and scree-slopes that plunged directly into the ocean. He was glad he hadn't tried to travel here by the more linear route over the ridges. He was less pleased that he would have to travel back the way he came, for there could be no safe route around the wide, beachless headland.

It was the very angularity of the landscape at this end of the island that led him to discover the storage facility. The building itself was well-concealed behind an extending arm of cliff, but it was given away by the unnaturally flat platform at the mouth of that hidden enclosure. Reaching the top of a jumbled pile of boulders, he spotted the platform at once, lying below him like a beacon. It was clearly a landing pad, and he felt a leap of excitement. He scrambled down the far side of the boulder pile, and picked his way towards the flattened area with as much haste as could be managed on a surface of slippery, shifting rocks. When he reached the pad, he bent down and placed his hands on it for a long and reverent moment: it was a connection with his fellow humanity, however tangential. Then he stood up and circled about, seeking the building that he knew instinctively would be somewhere nearby.

It didn't take him long to find it. The storage facility was a low, windowless bunker with its back and sides hard up against the containing cliffs. The door was sealed, of course, and he made several attempts to unlock it with his regular ident, his hand movements growing shakier and more urgent each time. Every effort was greeted with nothing more than the flashing of a small red light on the locking pad. At last he fell to beating on the featureless metal door with his fists, and then he collapsed to his knees and bellowed, the pent emotion of the past weeks finally bursting out of him, wild and overwhelming. Only when the frustration and grief were spent did he remember the emergency codes. Using them would set off alarms back at the main outpost – which might be his salvation, if his radio was merely broken, or might bring disaster if the base had fallen to some hostile force. Whatever the case, he knew there was no way he could simply turn around now and go back to the station without trying to find out what this bunker was, and what had happened to his colleagues. He barely hesitated before requesting an emergency code from his ident, and presenting it to the lock. This time, a yellow light lit up steadily and the door slid open.

The first thing he discovered in the rack-filled space was the food: endless boxes of freeze-dried provisions, just like the ones in the stores back at the station, only far more plentiful. Relieved by this unexpected bounty, he wasn't prepared for what he found in the rearmost rows of shelving. When he discovered the racks upon racks of weaponry and ammunition, his whole body constricted in an upsurge of rage. Their mission was scientific. The outpost on the far side of the globe, his agricultural station here on the island, they existed to study the planet, to assess its suitability for habitation. To find these filthy instruments of harm... How dare they? How dare they?

With his teeth clenched, he scoured the bunker for anything that might help him re-establish contact with the main outpost, but there was nothing. Eventually he slumped down against the bunker's smooth plascrete wall and tore open a ration pack. He ate it distractedly, barely tasting the balanced but utterly bland nutrition that was already far too familiar. He didn't know what the future would bring, but he knew what he had to do, and he would start tomorrow.

The bunker's provisioners had thoughtfully (if somewhat inexplicably) provided a carton of self-inflating dinghies. When he woke, after a poor night's sleep ridden with anxious dreams, he unpacked a dinghy and assessed the nearby coastline. The mountains' precipitous descent to the coast continued below the tide-line, and the sea became very deep within a short distance of the shore. He nodded to himself, then tethered his dinghy and returned to the bunker. He found a trolley, but decided it would be useless outside, on the surface of broken rock. Instead, armload by armload, he brought weapons and ammunition down to the dinghy, and when it was full, he paddled out to where the sea-floor was invisible. Then, gun following crate following canister, he dropped the items one by one over the side and watched with satisfaction as they plunged away into the cloudy alkaline depths. When the dinghy was empty, he paddled back to shore and did it again. And again. And again.

It became a rhythm—wake, eat, dump weapons – and he lost count of the days it took him to clear the weaponry out of the bunker, the number of cyclic voyages he took in the little inflatable. His body ached, his hands were blistered and his skin was cracked and weeping in places where the mildly caustic sea had repeatedly splashed it, but he kept on, his mind gripped by his anger, and by the necessity of doing *something*. When he finally departed on his return journey to the station, leaving the door wedged open by a large boulder and hauling as many ration-pouches as he could carry, he left behind him a storehouse that had been cleared of every scrap of militaria. Afterwards, when he thought back on this first visit to the bunker, he saw his actions as a kind of justified madness. They were the small but necessary protest of one far-flung man against the human folly that infested an entire galaxy.

It was only now, as an old and necessarily patient man, that he'd finally admitted his real reasons for coming to the station. When he signed up for the mission, he'd seen his enthusiasm as a last flush of late-youth optimism or pioneering spirit, a desire to help create a new and better place that could provide a home for a real community. Now, however, he could see that even as a younger man, he was already sickened by his own species and its seemingly inexhaustible capacity for tribalism and cruelty, for short-sighted greed. He'd come here to escape it all, to be alone – and if he ended up far more alone than he'd ever anticipated, perhaps it was really what he'd wished for all along. He had the bees and the apple trees, the twining potato plants and the elegant rows of corn that grew higher than his head. The island provided an exterior peace, and gradually, gently, he developed an inner peace to match it. He was content.

His breakfasting done, the man carried the bee-glass across to his work table, set it down and switched on the lamps. He charged up the whisker-like stunner, then tipped the bee onto the work surface and gave it a jolt to keep it still. The telescoping arm of the micro-manipulator array squeaked a little as he pulled it across in front of him, centering the camera on the bee before inserting his hands into the sensory gloves. These days, he used the maximum-inertia setting; he found that the resistance helped to compensate for the increasing tremor in his hands. He chose a wedge and a micro-tweezer and lowered them until they were just touching the bee. The magnifying screen and the gloves were so familiar to him now, had become such an extension of his own body, that their artifice immediately disappeared from his perception. It felt like he was working on a cat-sized insect with cutlery-sized tools.

Deftly, he slipped the wedge into the cleft where the bee's damaged wing met its body, and tilted it back and forth until it reached the correct angle. Then he took the micro-tweezer and grasped the wing near the base. In one smooth movement, he tweaked it out of the bee's thorax, then contemplated it with satisfaction: even when a wing was unsalvageable, it was still gratifying to remove it without damaging it further. He dropped the wing to one side, then tapped out the finger-code that opened the work table's sealed compartment. Here were his spare parts, some new, some scavenged from bees that had been damaged beyond repair: body shells, left and right wings, leg assemblies, pollination snouts, sensor arrays, processing units like crystalline grains of rice. It was ironic, really: his careful recycling meant that there were enough replacement parts here to keep the hive functioning long beyond the time when he'd be here to provide the repair service.

With the fine tweezers, he picked out a single wing, then drew it back towards the bee. Again, he used the wedge to open up the wing-joint, and then he maneuvered the wing into place, feeling it click home via the glove's sensitive haptics. The bee would be good as new. He pulled his hands out of the gloves and pushed the manipulator array aside. Having been out of the sunshine for a while, the bee would be low on power. He drew down the charge-lamp and switched it on, to give the bee a boost before he de-stunned it and returned it to its work – to its life.

He'd always thought of these tiny mechanical insects as having lives, however absurd the notion; they seemed no less living, and far more responsive to their environment, than the inert, floating rafts of algae-like micro-organisms that were this planet's only indigenous inhabitants. What would it be like to be reincarnated as an apple bee? He imagined it would be both purposeful and peaceful.

In the years of his Buddhist practice, he'd struggled with the whole concept of reincarnation – though the idea of karma seemed grimly self-evident, as humanity's increasing self-belligerence brought it nothing but suffering. Now, in the same way that long-submerged childhood memories had begun floating up into his mind, his adopted spirituality seemed to be giving way to snatches of his parents' religious teachings: a phrase here or there, the image of a garden, a fall from grace. He wondered, occasionally, if any of his family still lived; if any of his people, who had persecuted and been persecuted in turn, survived. Did any humans remain at all, apart from him? He had no way of knowing. Perhaps history was like an old man's mind, slowly turning back to where it came from, ending where it began; perhaps it was all just a long and repetitious madness, starting and ending with a fall.

He sat for a long time, looking out of the window at the hazy yellow sky while the bee charged up beneath the lamp. He'd long ago given up looking for approaching transports, but he still sometimes caught himself looking for clouds. If this planet had been blessed with any, he knew he'd have returned to one of his boyhood pursuits, spending happy hours lying on his back in the orchard, watching them drift across the sky, slowly changing shape from one fantastical form to another. Well, no matter. He could still close his eyes in the warm sunshine and remember them. The bee, too, would enjoy the sunshine, in its own micro-mechanical way. He picked up the stunner and gave the bee another tiny zap to de-stun it. Then, before the bee could take off, he cupped his hands around it and picked it up, enjoying the tickle as it buzzed within the small space between his palms. He walked to the main door, which slid away as he approached, and out onto the broad deck attached to the station, towards the thriving cultivations spread out in front of him.

The man paused at the railing and opened his hands, and the apple bee flew away, back towards the pastel-blossomed trees. He looked out over the long tracts of orchard, their healthy tapestry of pink and white and pale new green. *If it weren't for us, this place could have been a paradise,* he thought. Then he smiled, thinking of the bees he would leave behind. Until the last bee failed, and the orchard began its inevitable descent into senescence and death, the hive would continue in its sturdy labours, serving the spring blossom, bringing crops of perfect, forever-untasted apples to the trees. *It could have been a paradise,* he thought again. *And just for a little while, it will be.*

K.E. Macphee is an Australian writer now permanently settled in Scotland, whose lifelong enthusiasm for short-form SF has inspired a career in computing and digital media, with detours through robotics, machine vision and astronomy. This elusive creature can sometimes be glimpsed on Highlands backroads, perched atop an insect-spattered motorcycle and sporting a very big grin.

Satellite 6

...some like it hot

Three days of Science Fiction, Science Fact, and Science Fun

Guest of Honour
Paul McAuley

Crowne Plaza Hotel, Glasgow
25th — 27th May, 2018
http://Six.SatelliteX.org.uk

Don't Speak; Don't Listen

Serena Johe

Art: Sara Julia

It's always our fault, whoever we are. I can't be the only one tired of hearing this frip. Before the Mods it was the VR, before the VR it was Pakbots, the Holos, the NMedia, all the way back to the "internet." And before that, I'm sure it was cellphones and telephones and cars and carrier pigeons, too. Technology always ruins civilization as we know it. Young people always destroy the integrity of our values.

What. Ever. It's so easy to blame the frip that's happening in front of you and forget about the people that put it there. Newsflash: that was you. Deal with it. Don't like what I have to say? Wops to you, sister.

My aunt, for example, litz grabbed my arm to keep me from heading to the shop to tat it up with the rest of the country. Puh-lease. Everyone and their mother's getting a LYB – everyone with morals, anyway – so why the plick shouldn't I? But Auntie practically begged me not to get one. She even cursed. And I'm talking old-world style, like the 'f-word', and I don't mean 'frip.' She needs a LYB more than I do, if you ask me.

I wound up waiting in line for three hours outside the tat shop, enduring the unbearable humidity and the heat trapped downtown. Towers edge the streets from corner to corner. The shop takes up the bottom two floors of one of the gigantor buildings. Their holo sign projects over the entire storefront, a vibrant amalgamation of their latest work in styles from surrealist, to tribal, to new-neo-Japanese. They're one of the biggest in town, and by far the best. More than good enough to back up their flashiness and explain the enormous line.

The capacity monitor allowed two more people past the entrance, and the lot of us eagerly scuttled forward. I was close enough now to see two Jacks practically skip out the door.

"Hey!" I waved to get their attention. They stopped mid-step, so fast one of the Jack's clawed feet raked against the pavement.

He nudged the other Jack in the ribs, and they both turned to me, smiling. "What's going down, Jill?"

"You get a LYB?"

"Wouldn't be here otherwise." They both stuck out their tongues to show off the tiny script, two letters centered in the jagged symbol for leptosexual rights. Their LYBs matched.

"Stacked," I grinned at them.

"You think? Check this out." One of the Jacks turned to the other. I saw his mouth move to form the beginning of a derogatory word – either gibber, or something worse, an old world insult – but then his lips twitched and his tongue stiffened in his mouth. The LYB shimmered slightly, like someone shined a light from one end to the other, as it communicated with the surrounding LYBs. He couldn't say the word.

"Now that," I amended, "is stacked."

The people in line around me muttered their agreement. We suddenly found ourselves a lot less irate. I looked around and met the eyes of mods, leptos, queers, scalers, skin in every hue and faces in every shape, and I imagined that they, like me, were reminded of our conviction: to free ourselves and others from the constraints of our own prejudice. It was a rare moment of camaraderie in an ever-divided society.

Do me a favor. Imagine a world in which we couldn't hurt each other, where any person – from transparent to black, from scaled to furred – could walk down the street without fear of rebuke or harassment.

That was our goal, and that's why we gathered there. To be liberators.

I just wished Auntie could understand that.

I didn't know what design I wanted for my LYB when I left the house that day, but the three-and-a-half hour wait gave me plenty of time to think about it. I figured I'd get something simple, something timeless. Showy frip has never been my scene. My tats are old-style, black-and-white, none of that 3D or temperature sensitive stuff. I settled on a black equal sign. Simple and to the point. The artist clamped my tongue, drew the stamp, and twenty minutes later, it was done.

Now, I thought, to show it off. I went home and snuck past my aunt, snagging the VR helmet on my way to my bedroom. I knew Stella would be in class re-watching our lecture. Our university only uses the immersive programs, and I had to flip the settings through three different lecture halls before I found her in bio class tapping away at the system files.

She turned around, clearly grunged at my unannounced poke in the shoulder, but her face lit up when she saw my LYB. "You got one!"

"Obvi," I snarked, but it came out more like 'omfi' with my tongue still hanging out of my mouth.

Stella paused the professor so we could hear each other. "Nice," she nodded, admiring the simple design, "it suits you."

I pulled my tongue back into my mouth and couldn't keep from smiling. "Thanks. Now we're both ready for the march. You're still meeting me there, right?"

"Duh!" Stella rolled her eyes. "That's still two months away, though. Can you survive that long with your aunt grunging you all the time?"

"She's not that bad."

"Kaley."

"Seriously!" I defended. "She's the sweetest person I know. She just doesn't like to show it."

Stella looked ready to argue, but someone else loaded into the classroom. Study date, if I had to guess.

"Talk soon?" I winked at her. She rolled her eyes again, and I disconnected the VR. I'd tease her about it later.

When I approached Auntie that evening as she unmolded our dinner, she didn't say a word about my LYB. She's always vocal about her opinions – no matter how vulgar or how inappropriate the context – and I had to pinch myself when she didn't berate me for following through with the mod. She just shook her head and muttered.

I took it as a sign that everything would turn out all right. Maybe she'd had a change of heart, or maybe she just knew arguing wouldn't amount to anything. I'd already gone and done it, after all.

Gladly avoiding any unpleasant confrontations, I passed the next few weeks catching up on classes and cycling through the newly loaded NVO's on the VR. Thousands of rooms exist on the city's intersystem. I killed a lot of time jumping from one to the next, sometimes to rather unsavory places. At least a few times I loaded into segregationist rooms, "non-mod" only, virtual conservative houses of worship. No sooner than I appeared, the rooms went silent. They didn't have to speak to let me know I wasn't welcome.

Where there are people, there is hatred. I don't understand how anyone justifies their prejudice like that, and I didn't bother to stay and find out.

But, on the bright side, as I scrolled through the list of newly crafted NVO's, I found a frip-ton dedicated to LYBers. I loaded into exotic rooms, beaches that I'd never seen in the physical world, houses of people I'd never met, and found myself surrounded by people who thought like me, who believed in the same things. In the face of my aunt's silent disapproval, these rooms reminded me of why I'd gotten the mod in the first place.

My LYB didn't activate during my NVO jumping, though, and neither did anyone else's. Mostly, those of us who had them were likeminded. We had little chance of offending each other, but Stella saw it at least once. When we met at our favorite NVO – a fire-warmed log cabin in New Hampshire, when the White Mountain National Forest still stood circa 2041 – we both balked at the idiocy of our classmates. Our university hosted an annual physical event, and of course that's always asking for it with a group of volatile, opinionated teenagers.

"So, what was his plan, exactly?" I asked after she finished recounting the scene. "And why the plick did he think it would work?"

Stella shook her head and shrugged. "I guess he figured pulling the 'man' card would earn him some points with the male debate judges."

"Seriously, what century does he think he's in? I wish I could've seen his face when his LYB went off."

"Oh, yeah," she grinned around the lip of her coffee mug, "it was priceless. He looked beyond grunged."

"I can imagine." Serves him right, I thought. I pictured it in my head – his attempted sexist remark, the look on his face, the anger. He probably didn't even realize he'd been about to say something offensive, which is exactly why the LYBs come in handy. They beat down ignorance before it can rear its ugly head.

Everything about it felt justified. I could hardly imagine a more fitting application for a LYB than an academic debate, but the more I thought about his face getting all gnarly, the more something nagged at me.

I nudged Stella under the table to tear her attention from the window. She'd set the NVO to blizzard.

"Hey, why do you think a guy like that got a LYB in the first place?"

"What do you mean?"

"Like, maybe he didn't know he'd been about to say something sexist, right?" Stella appeared skeptical, but I continued before she could argue, "Either way, if he really thinks that men have more legit opinions than women, why would he have gotten something that prevented him from spewing that frip?"

"Plick if I know." She didn't seem concerned about it, but I knew it must've bothered her a little bit by the way she didn't immediately turn back to the window. "Almost everyone in our classes has a LYB now. I doubt they're all socially enlightened."

"Good point," I admitted. It would be terribly unlikely for every single person in our university to be that self-aware, wouldn't it? "You don't think," I started doubtfully, "that he got one because he's offended by feminism, do you?"

Stella laughed incredulously. "What? How would that work?"

"Like, so he doesn't have to hear about it from anyone. The LYB would prevent people from talking to him about it, if it really offended him."

"That's a load of frip. He's the one that's insulting people."

"Yeah, but that means it has to work both ways, doesn't it?"

Stella frowned at the ceiling. "Whatever. He's still wrong." She turned to face the window, and we both watched the snowfall in silence.

Our conversation bothered me. I concluded my uneasiness had to do with how I hadn't personally seen the LYBs in action yet, but I'd get my chance soon enough at the Mod's Rights March. Rumors of a counter-protest lurked on the intersystem, and I seriously doubted the MRM would happen seamlessly, considering.

In the meantime, I immersed myself in the preparations. Organizing for the march proved a good enough distraction from any doubts I may have had – maybe too much so. I logged nearly eighty hours on the VR over the next month just trying to keep up with meetings. As a member of the senior student council, many of the responsibilities for planning university related demonstrations fell on my shoulders, and it took me two weeks to come up with a reliable method of transportation that fit within the skimpy budget. Just when I thought we'd finally found a way to haul four thousand students from point A to point B, the VP informed me that the bus company I'd planned to use was staunchly anti-mod. The irony did not amuse me.

My aunt couldn't have missed my chronic irritation with the mess. I spent a good deal of time pacing the living room floor and doing fruitless calculations on my AR implant. I probably looked like a mad person, dragging my feet across the carpet and angrily swiping my hands through the air like I'd been swarmed by mosquitoes.

"What's eating you?" she finally asked. "It's like you've been PMSing for a month straight."

She'd just come back from the store, and reflexively, I helped her carry bags into the kitchen and unload them. "As if there couldn't be any other reason I'd be upset, since I'm a woman."

"Well, I wouldn't have any idea, seeing as I'm not a woman," she grumbled, her tone oozing sarcasm. "It's an expression, Kaley. I didn't mean to offend your delicate sensibilities."

She said the word "offend" like some kind of insult. I paused with my hand on the refrigerator door, thoroughly confused. As prickly as Auntie could be, she rarely got legit angry. "What's eating *you?*"

"You are," she snapped. She practically threw the box of salt into the cabinet, nearly toppling the whole spice rack. "You know I can't go anywhere anymore without someone talking my ear off about this damn mods-rights LYB shit?"

"We're just trying to help, Auntie. We're –"

"Don't," she interrupted, holding her hand up. "Don't you say it. You can go liberate yourselves all you like, and you can use whatever backwards logic you damn well please, but I don't want any part in it. If I never hear that word again, it'd be too soon."

My heart dropped. "Don't tell me you're anti-mod now."

"I'm not anti anything," she grumbled, much to my relief. "And I'm not pro anything, either. People should do whatever the hell they want."

"So, then, what's the problem? Nobody's forcing you to support anything, you know."

Auntie dropped the bag of coffee on the shelf and turned to look at me. She propped her hip against the edge of the counter and narrowed her eyes in that particular scrutinizing way that always makes me feel like an idiot. I tried not to fidget. "When was the last time you've been outside?"

"I've been –"

"Not the VR. I mean physically outside. You know," she lowered her voice to annunciate the point, "places you're not surrounded by people that agree with you all the time?"

Now I couldn't help but fidget. When was the last time I'd physically left the house? I couldn't remember. I'd been so caught up in schoolwork and MRM prep that the thought hadn't even occurred to me.

"I don't know," I admitted. "Not since I got my LYB, I guess. But how bad could it be?"

She stared at me for a long, tense moment. Then she pushed herself off the counter and turned back to the groceries. I didn't have to see her face to know the disappointment I'd find there.

She spoke calmly. "I love you, Kaley, but right now, you've got your head so far up your ass all you can hear is your own echo."

Auntie's irritability got worse as the date of the march got closer. I wondered why she even did her errands in the tangible world since everyone grunged her so badly, but when I suggested that she simply save herself the trouble, she didn't take it well. "You know what?" she snapped, "Fine."

Then she left the house anyway.

After sitting alone in agitated confusion for nearly an hour, I followed her out the door and wandered downtown to look for her. I halfway expected to find mass pandemonium – burning cars, looters, desecration of Mod's rights flags, anything that might justify her anger, but I found the city still standing and its people the typical degree of non-homicidal. It took me nearly two hours to locate what I thought must be the source of Auntie's chagrin.

It was the only anomalous thing I saw, at least, but I couldn't make sense of it: six solemn looking protestors on the corner of 6th and F St. They bore the usual anti-mod slogans on their posters – appeals to nature, "perfect the way we are," that sort of jargon. The oddity came in the form of the Jill sitting on the sidewalk in front of them. Not a protestor, as far as I could tell. She carried no sign, and even from across the street, I saw the slant of her reptilian eyes, the short crown of gator scales on her elbows. A mod.

I couldn't figure out what about this might've upset my aunt so badly. Their silence surely didn't count as "getting an earful." Wearily, I crossed the street.

"Hey," I greeted. The Jill glanced up at me and raised one feathered eyebrow. "What's going on?"

She jabbed a thumb over her shoulder at the protestors. "They were screaming anti-mod – stuff," she amended the almost-curse. A LYB flashed on her tongue.

That much made sense. "Okay, so, you're counter-protesting, or what?"

"Sort of."

"Sort of?"

She shrugged. "I'm shutting them up, at least."

The Jack at the front of the protest group frowned. His eyes slid over to me, one slightly slower than the other. An impairment – something a mod might easily fix. Not that he'd ever consider it. He caught me staring and glared. I expected him to open his mouth and unleash a fresh wave of sloganized nonsense, but he remained tight-lipped. It wasn't hard to figure out why.

"Wait," I glanced back and forth between them and the Jill, "they have LYBs too?"

"Obvi."

"What? Why? They're supposed to be anti-mod – anti-LYB."

The Jill cocked her head at me. She sounded annoyed by my apparent ignorance. "There are legit millions of us. They probs thought that keeping us quiet would be more effective than arguing."

"How can they expect to change anyone's mind about mods if they have one? That doesn't make a plick of sense." I waited for the anti-mods to say something, but they still wouldn't talk. But maybe that was the whole idea. Even if they couldn't convince us, they could still keep us from fighting for our cause. Maybe this was their sacrifice for theirs. I remembered my conversation with Stella. "That's not the point of a LYB. We're the ones that are fighting for –"

Equality, was what I meant to say. My tongue deadened in my mouth. I couldn't finish the thought, and in disbelief, I stared slack-jawed at the smug faces of the protestors.

Many of these street demonstrations must've cropped up in response to the MRM, though I doubted most people spent their time silencing them like this Jill had. Auntie must've passed small-scale protests like this for the last month and been forced to endure them as one of increasingly fewer people without a LYB. Immediately, I understood where she'd stormed off to.

I only made it a few steps before the Jack called after me. Hesitantly, not trusting my mouth yet in its strange state of numbness, I turned around and waited.

"Are you going to the march?" he asked. I nodded, and he grinned in a way I found distinctly unfriendly. "I'll see you there."

The line outside the tat shop spanned a full two blocks now. Something else had changed, too. As I scanned the faces of the people in line, I didn't find the same representative diversity of our city. Or, not completely. The scalers and queers and leptos were still there, the feathered plumes and the furry ears still rose above the crowd, but threaded amongst them stood the unadulterated bodies of dozens of anti-modders.

Anti-modders in line. To get a mod.

I wanted to point it out to them, to show them how ridiculous it was, but I didn't dare. The tension palpated between bodies like a current. Nobody spoke. They stared as I passed them, scrutinizing my tattoos – plain enough to be unmodded, plentiful enough to make that unlikely. Their pupils rolled to the corners of their eyes as if afraid of meeting mine, but I felt them staring all the same, mods and anti-mods alike, trying to figure out which side I was on.

It didn't make sense. The line I'd stood in to get my LYB had been impatient, but not hostile, for plick's sake.

I found Auntie towards the entrance. Only a dozen people stood in front of her in the queue. The silence felt so complete that I approached her whispering. "Auntie, what the plick are you doing?"

She shrugged. "Exactly what you said. Saving myself the trouble."

"This isn't what I meant," I hissed back. "I meant you should just shop by VR or IS, not do this. You don't want a LYB – you don't even have any mods!" The Jack in front of her, an obvious sparker judging by the stylized machinery of his right half, looked over his shoulder at my aunt and scoffed.

I couldn't help it. I snapped. "What the hell is your problem?"

He had no facial hair, no eyebrows to raise. He simply turned and stared.

"We're supposed to be fighting for our differences," I pressed, unperturbed by his stoic expression and the fiberglass on his skin. "Not to frip all over everyone else's!"

"Tell that to your friend there."

"She's my aunt, and for your information," I started, ready to let him have it, but I could only watch in bottled indignation as he turned away and conspicuously hit the mute button by his ear.

"Kaley," Auntie sighed. "Just forget it."

"I can't just forget it! You're not an anti-mod, or a bigot, or – whatever. A little tactless, maybe," I conceded, "but you're still the kindest person I know."

The corner of her mouth quirked into a rueful half-smile. "I know I'm not a bigot. He's just going to keep thinking I am until I get a mod."

"But – you can't seriously be considering this," I insisted. "Even if you did get one, then anti-mods would assume you're a bigot for getting one. It doesn't make any sense."

"No, it doesn't." She acknowledged it with the resigned nonchalance of someone who's already gone a hundred miles in the wrong direction. "But at least now I won't have to hear about it."

I still went to the march, if only to support the mods. What else could I do? I'd organized for it, obligated myself to lead parts of it, and promised Stella I'd meet here there for the first time in person. I had to go.

It went, more or less, as I expected. The mods and anti-mods faced off across a line of protective police, each side nearly ten thousand strong, and each crowd turned inward, as if we weren't a few yards from each other. We talked amongst ourselves, held our signs high, whispered. The tension built and amounted to nothing, just hung there in the air between us and amongst us, thick as syrup.

There were supposed to be speakers. Twelve in total, six for each side, but they took the stage and none of them could say a word.

Serena Johe is an avid reader and writer with a particular interest in speculative fiction. Her work appears or is forthcoming in publications such as *Typehouse*, *Chantwood Magazine*, *The Forge*, *Schlock!*, *The Colored Lens*, *FLAPPERHOUSE*, and *Five on the Fifth*, amongst others.

And the Winner Is...

In Shoreline of Infinity 8, published in June 2017, we announced our first flash fiction competition, and over the summer months you all took to the beaches with your pads and pencils and came up with some delightful wee science fiction stories. Many thanks to all of you who were inspired by Becca McCall's and Siobhan McDonald's artwork, and entertained us in the Autumnal chill of October.

Shoreline of Infinity was honoured when Pippa Goldschmidt and Eric Brown accepted our invitation to act as judges, and as you will read in their reports, they enjoyed their task with relish – many thanks for your efforts, Eric and Pippa.

Without further ado, we present...

Art: Siobhan McDonald

A Choice for the Golden Age

Matthew Castle

WINNER
Shoreline of Infinity Flash Fiction
Competition 2017

The **Captain wakes**, reborn into the *Golden Age* for the sixteenth time.

"Welcome back, sister," says Ship. "We're nearly there."

Aiko's eyes snap into focus. She recognises Ship's voice, her immediate surroundings, and the same old sequence of sensation and thought that has followed each of her embodiments to date. The unnerving sharpness in the lines and corners of the printing chamber's ceiling, the tickle of an air current on her cheek, and the never-answered question that bursts into her mind each time: I am awake, but am I alive?

Even as she flexes each new finger and waggles each new toe, she explores her wider sensorium, evaluating the status of the *Golden Age*: the ship, the crew, the sleepers, and the progress of the journey.

She swings her legs off the fabrication table and takes two cautious steps towards the mirrored hatch. She looks herself up and down, and giggles: she is a child. Short, shiny-skinned, narrow-jointed and unmistakably non-biological, but elegant nonetheless. She estimates her mass to be around eighteen percent less than the last time she was embodied, which was – as she forms the question, Ship soundlessly supplies the answer – eight hundred and sixty three years ago. She's smaller and a little less human each time she wakes.

"Guess we're really pushing against matter-energy constraints now," she says aloud, testing the sound of her voice. It is a simple electronic speaker system this time, and the tone is high and piping. She giggles again, like tinkling water. She was always a good talker. She'll never need to stop for breath again.

"We've had to consume significant reaction mass in course adjustments," says Ship. "And most systems are approaching their resilience thresholds. We've had a number of closed loop failures. Non-linearities are proliferating. And there's a choice to be made. That's why the voyagers wanted you back, rather than the rostered primary crewmember. The *Golden Age* needs its captain."

Aiko nods. She reaches for the hatch, but stops suddenly, and gasps.

"What is it, Aiko?" asks Ship.

"A dream. I was dreaming."

There are several types of sleeper on the *Golden Age*. At any one time there are two or three active human crew. Their primary role, other than maintaining biological continuity, is to manage the ship's zoo and gardens. They grow and eat food, make love, raise children, and sleep and dream in the age-old way.

And there are the cold sleepers, the two hundred-odd descendants or surrogated offspring of the original crew, whose metabolism has been slowed to a crawl by cryoprotectants and ever-more tenuously preserved hibernation technology. A complex Ship-devised algorithm rotates them out of cold sleep at an optimal premenopausal moment, and suggests when to rotate their adolescent children back into hibernation, taking numerous parameters – including physical and personal developmental milestones and ship resource constraints – into some unknowable account. Cold sleepers dream, but never remember.

Then there are many thousands of gametes, frozen boilerplate embryos, and whole-person encodable genome sequences. Less than thirty percent of the embryos remain viable after a dozen millennia, but that still leaves a veritable treasure trove of human diversity. It is the sleep of possibility; a dreamless resting potential.

Finally, there are the uploaded: the preserved mind states of former crew. Ship's network storage substrate is a finite resource, and a human mind takes up a lot of space, so not everyone gets uploaded. The *Golden Age*'s original crew are permitted this privilege, as they form a vital first-hand link with the terrestrial culture that built and launched the *Golden Age*. Usually, at least one avatar-embodied mind state is active at any one time, passing knowledge and traditions to the newer generations. Between embodiments, the uploaded crew consume few resources, evolving at a glacial pace: the minimum required for self-coherence.

Ship's avatar meets Aiko outside the printing chamber.

"We'll go straight to the viewing gantry," Ship says. "You can tell me about your dream on the way."

Ship is a metallic skinned human-sized figure motionless in repose, but implacable in motion. Aiko glides smoothly, despite her toy-like appearance.

"I've never dreamed in upload before." The metal floors are worn and the walls are thinner than Aiko remembers; the *Golden Age* is consuming herself as she nears the end of her voyage. "There's a door at the end of a curving wooden walkway. Water laps underneath." She tries to slow down, but her little legs appear to be slaved to Ship's long, relentless stride. "There are plants in the windows. Someone is waiting."

They emerge onto the viewing gantry, and join a small family.

There's a man. He wears hooded coveralls with soil-stains on the knees and elbows. There's a woman, and a boy. Two males: earlier generations of crew would have regarded this as wastefully suboptimal. She reviews their life histories again: they're good people. But they seem nervous, today.

"We're honoured by your embodiment, Grandmother-Captain," says the woman. She looks confused; perhaps wondering why Ship made Aiko so small.

"We are at an important point in our journey," Aiko says, "and a decision needs to be made."

Aiko gazes out. A globe fills the screen. It's a representation of a terrestrial planet situated in the habitable zone of the K class star Groombridge 1618: their destination.

In most respects, Ship is the real master of the *Golden Age*, of course. But for now, there is still a former human in the loop.

It's a simple binary decision. Decelerating will consume over half the mass of the *Golden Age*. If human biological continuity is to be maintained, all that clunky, hopelessly outdated wetware and its associated supporting paraphernalia – the cold sleepers, the gametes, the embryos and the crispvats – must be preserved. Weighed against that is a future refined and optimised over many centuries of travel: the processing substrate that hosts Ship's Mind, and the minds of all Aiko's old crewmates.

The Captain remembers the rest of her dream, and chooses.

Matthew Castle lives in the south of England. He works in the NHS by day, and writes speculative fiction and narrative non-fiction by night

Judge's Report

Eric Brown

I've heard horror stories about being the judge of literary contests; Booker Prize committees coming to blows; the Whitbread judges falling out and never speaking to each other again; division among the Nobel Prize committee causing lasting enmity… Well, glad to report, the judging of the flash-fiction competition run by the Scottish SF magazine *Shoreline of Infinity* posed none of the above pitfalls. Pippa Goldschmidt and I, ably assisted by Shoreline's editor Noel Chidwick, had a

pleasurable time reading through the eighty-one submitted stories and narrowing them down to a long-list of twelve.

So, what were we looking for in our winners?

We wanted stories that were well-written – that was a given – original, concise, and with as much characterisation as the author might manage in the restricted word limit of just 1k. A tall order.

We decided between us to whittle the entries down to a favourite dozen, with ten or so follow-ups. That was relatively easy. Of the eighty-one stories, I'd say that about thirty were of a standard suitable for publication, a higher proportion than I was expecting. For me, some stories stood out… The thing was, would my fellow judges agree?

We exchanged a list of our dozen favourites simultaneously by email at ten o'clock one Monday morning, and I admit I was a little chagrined to find that the other judges agreed with only three of my dozen, though many of them appeared on their follow-up lists.

The disparity made me go though their lists, re-read and re-assess their favoured stories, and realise that on a third and fourth reading I appreciated aspects of these tales that had eluded me on my first and second readings.

Pippa and Noel came down to my house in the Borders for lunch – Noel bringing his red setter Rosa to meet my red and white setter, Uther – and a walk on the beach afterwards.

But first the business of agreeing on a short-list of six best tales, and then the top three, and a winner...

Over coffee we discussed the merits and demerits of around forty stories, speaking up for our favourites and criticising others. What I found instructive about the process was the critical insight brought by Noel and Pippa, which in many instances made me reassess my opinion of certain stories.

I thought the standard of the top twelve very high indeed, and the top six would have graced the pages of many a professional magazine. Thankfully we were in broad agreement about the six, the top three, and the story which we agreed was the winner. (And, amazingly, we didn't resort to arm-wrestling to settle the matter.)

The experience taught me a few things: that there are many talented writers out there; that the short form of the SF genre is fit and healthy; and that good stories get better with multiple readings.

(And, if you're wondering, Uther and Rosa did enjoy each others' company and had a fine time romping on the beach).

Eric Brown has a long list of science fiction books to his name. He won the British Science Fiction Award twice for his short stories, and his novel *Helix Wars* was shortlisted for the 2012 Philip K. Dick award.
His latest releases are *Murder Take Three* and *Binary System*. He writes a regular science fiction review column for the Guardian newspaper and lives in Cockburnspath, Scotland.
His website can be found at: www.ericbrown.co.uk

Judge's Report

Pippa Goldschmidt

Reading other people's writing is necessarily a subjective business, so how does the process of judging work? To some extent, it does depend on a 'gut feeling' – 'do I like this story?' but it also depends on whether I think it works. The three basic questions I ask of any piece of writing are 'what is it trying to do?', 'does it succeed in doing this?' and 'is this an interesting thing to do?'

Correspondingly, a competition judge has a responsibility to ensure they approach each short story with the same mind-set so they are judging it in the same way as all the others; I think there is a requirement to be open and willing to be engaged, and on the flip side to have a sharp eye able to spot any weaknesses or flaws.

And it's a big ask to deliver a satisfactory short story in less than a thousand words. I think we were prepared to forgive some flaws if we could be persuaded that there was enough to compensate.

So, I sat down on the sofa one weekend afternoon and resolved to read all short stories in one go. I almost did it, but a gin and tonic called me away towards the end.

I made a long long-list and then a shorter one. I scribbled 'maybe' next to several stories.

I went back and re-read and re-read again.

Some stories could be ruled out from the start. They made the info-dump mistake, giving the reader too much information in a manner that distracted from the story's momentum.

Many years of writing short stories has taught me that they can only stand a very small amount of info-dumping.

Some stories read more like the interesting beginnings to longer pieces of work. They set up the premise but then failed to deliver any sort of resolution.

Other stories were set in a future with whizz bang technologies, and yet curiously the societies themselves had not changed from today's. But the huge strength and power of SF lies in its abilities to imagine future societies. So those stories were rejected too.

Even after I'd wielded the rejection pen, there were a satisfyingly large number that I was still interested in. I made my final long-list which loosely corresponded to Eric's and Noel's. That's the advantage of having more than one judge – we would now have to argue our choices and articulate just what we thought worked and didn't work. We would have to persuade each other about our favourites.

This process worked well. We sat in Eric's living room and talked and talked. We scrabbled around amongst piles of papers and recalcitrant laptops. The household pets got involved (Uther howled at us periodically and the cats sat on the papers).

We had a break for lunch and returned to the fray; there was a degree of compromise in the final list (there always is) but we were all happy with it. Then we went to the beach.

Pippa Goldschmidt is the author of the novel *The Falling Sky* and the short story collection *The Need for Better Regulation of Outer Space*. In 2016, she was a winner of the MRC Suffrage Science award and her poem 'Physics for unwary students' was chosen to be one of the Scottish Poetry Library's Best Scottish Poems.

Pippa is a regular at Shoreline of Infinity's Event Horizon.

Virtually, Pippa lives at: www.pippagoldschmidt.co.uk

The Worthy Winners

The judges left us their notes on the shortlist of 6:

1) "A Choice for the Golden Age" by Matthew Castle.
A worthy winner of the contest.

A powerful story which is not only original, but manages to pose a poignant dilemma with the closing lines. I couldn't fault the writing; it's tight, economical and professional. I particularly liked the way the author managed to convey a lot of background information without recourse to info dumps. Like all good tales, it managed to suggest a greater universe going on behind what was presented.

Runner-up) "ATU334 the Wise" by Marija Smit.

Neat up-dating of the Slavic Baba Yaga folk tale of a witch with chicken legs, helping those she comes across, or not... It's economically told, light and amusing – suggesting that even the oldest of myths will survive in the far-future. It's also the perfect length, suggesting an author in full control of her material.

Runner-up) "Pauline and the Bahnians" by S. K. Farrell.

A strong story told in an epistolary format of a homesteader writing to a bolshy military commander. I liked the unusual background here – how many SF stories manage to mention Orpington chickens? – and the tongue-in-cheek humour.

Shortlist) "A Modest Proposal" by Art Lasky.

Humour isn't easy to achieve in SF, and harder still in just seven hundred words. Lasky made me laugh three times in the first page. It's a simple story well told, with a couple of neat twists built around a clever idea. The early plant, with the repulsive alien stating: "I find the thought of probing something disgusting as a human repulsive..." is mirrored nicely in the pay-off. And the twist is lovely.

Shortlist) "In the Rose Garden" by Maria Haskins.

This story manages to suggest a lot in a very short space. As economical a tone-poem, and as sensitively observed, it's not only a sad retrospective reflection on one man's – or rather being's – failed hopes for his adopted planet, but an exploration of loneliness, isolation, and hope for the future.

Shortlist) "The Quantum Window" by Laura Duerr.

A well-written account of a school trip to see the Quantum Window, a portal high above Earth that gives glimpses of our planet in alternate realities.

The Longlist:

Cammie Campbell, Seeking Water, Seeking Sky

DS Camperdown, The Last Enchantment

Matthew Castle, A Choice for the Golden Age

Barry Charman, Matter

Neil Chue Hong, Time Of My Life

Laura Duerr, The Quantum Window

SK Farrell, Pauline and the Bahnians

Simon Fung, A Game of Dolls

Kirsty Hammond, Glorious

Maria Haskins, In The Rose Garden

Art Lasky, A Modest Proposal

Katie Gray, My House

Brian M. Milton,The Oculus at the Edge of the Universe

Marija Smits, ATU334 The Wise

These stories will be published in a collection to appear in 2018.

Well done everyone, and thanks to all who sent us stories.

We will be repeating this competition in 2018, so sharpen those pencils.

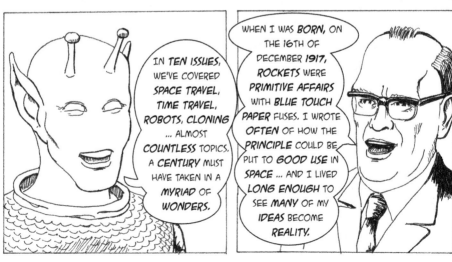

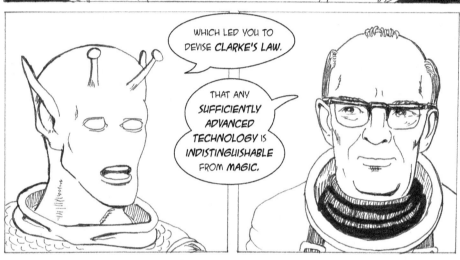

2016 ARTHUR C CLARKE AWARDS
INNOVATOR: MR. JEFFREY P. BEZOS,
AMAZON.COM
IMAGINATION IN SERVICE TO SOCIETY: MR.
BRAN FERREN, APPLIED MINDS
LIFETIME ACHIEVEMENT: THE NATIONAL
AERONAUTICAL AND SPACE
ADMINISTRATION (NASA)

2015 ARTHUR C. CLARKE AWARDS
INNOVATOR: GREG WYLER, ONEWEB
AND O3B
IMAGINATION IN SERVICE TO SOCIETY:
MARGARET ATWOOD, CANADIAN POET,
NOVELIST, LITERARY CRITIC, AND
ENVIRONMENTAL ACTIVIST
LIFETIME ACHIEVEMENT: LOCKHEED
MARTIN'S SKUNK WORKS

2014 ARTHUR C CLARKE AWARDS
LIFETIME ACHIEVEMENT: HON. NORMAN
AUGUSTINE
INNOVATOR AWARD: SKYBOX IMAGING
IMPACT OF IMAGINATION ON SOCIETY:
LARRY NIVEN
AUTHOR OF SCIENCE FICTION AND
FANTASY WORKS

Interview: Helen Sedgwick

In conversation with **Pippa Goldschmidt**

Helen has an MLitt in Creative Writing from Glasgow University and has won a Scottish Book Trust New Writers Award. Her debut novel *The Comet Seekers* has been published in seven countries including the UK, US and Canada, it got rave reviews in many different newspapers including The New York Times and was selected as one of the best books of **2016** by The Herald and Glamour. *The Comet Seekers* weaves together science and fantasy to tell the story of two people whose tale is told through glimpses of a comet reappearing throughout history.

As a literary editor, Helen has worked as the managing director of Cargo Publishing and managing editor of Gutter, and she founded Wildland Literary Editors in 2012. Before that, Helen was a research physicist with a PhD in Physics from Edinburgh University.

Helen's second novel *The Growing Season* was recently published by Harvill Secker. This novel is set in the near future when it is the norm for babies to develop in artificial wombs that are provided by a private company. Now both men and women can truly share 'pregnancy', is this the end of female inequality?

Pippa Goldschmidt: You're known as a writer who's an ex-scientist and who explores the world of science in your novels. Did you always want to be a writer? How did you move from science to literature?

Helen Sedgwick: I don't think it occurred to me that 'being a writer' was a thing you could actually do, when I was younger. Writing was never on my list of potential careers when I was at school, and I moved away from English and languages to focus on science and music as soon as I could. All through university and my 20s I didn't write at all – it didn't really cross my mind to try. Which is strange really, given that I read all the time and always have.

It wasn't until I was approaching 30 that I started an evening class in creative writing – and even then my focus wasn't on writing so much as finding something new. I actually took classes in Indian dance, life drawing, French, Thai cookery, pretty much anything I could think of! But it was in the creative writing class that I think I found what I was looking for. During that course I started work on my first novel – I kind of skipped right over short stores and just began writing a book. The first few chapters of that (still and always to remain unpublished)

© Michael Gallacher

novel made up my application to the MLitt in Creative Writing at Glasgow University. I was working at the university in the bio-electronics group at the time, so I was able to go part time in my postdoc and then take the MLitt simultaneously. By the end of that year, I knew writing was what I wanted to do.

PG: How do you approach a new project? Do you start off with the characters or a scientific question that you want to write about?

HS: With *The Growing Season* that's certainly how it started – I wanted to write about biotechnology and feminism, and the idea of the baby pouch (a portable, artificial womb) was the

THE GROWING SEASON

HELEN SEDGWICK

natural overlap. I don't think the scientific idea came on its own though, it was very much about how society responds to technology, how a scientific invention can impact our world. I often try to explore scientific ideas by putting them in a human, hopefully relatable context. For *The Comet Seekers*, I took the idea of a comet's orbit and tried to show human lives representing that, with the idea of home or belonging as the centre point – the Sun – that the characters can never quite reach but never escape either.

I've got an idea for a book about quantum entanglement next, so I'm currently trying to work out how human lives can be connected across space and time in a way that might illustrate that paradox. But then I've also just finished my first draft of a crime book about aliens – so it's not all serious!

For me, there's also a big element of just following the story and characters where they lead. I'm not a big planner. I tend to start with an idea that I want to explore and a central relationship that I'm going to explore it through. I then develop an idea of where that starts and finishes – often by writing the final scene first – so I have a rough character arc in mind and a sense of where the story is headed. And then I start writing and see what happens! It's a process that seems to give me a lot of momentum when I'm writing a first draft, and also results in years of editing to get the book into shape afterwards. I enjoy editing almost as much as writing itself (although I think it uses a very different part of the brain) so it's a process that seems to work for me. Every book is different though, and I never really know how the next one is going to go.

PG: Working as a scientist involves a rigorous process and implies an impartiality to the subject matter under scrutiny whereas writing fiction gives you a certain amount of latitude – you can make up your whole fictional universe!

Do you think there are any commonalities between doing science and writing?

HS: The frustration? That's a joke, don't put that in! Or maybe you should... There are many things that science and writing have in common, but perhaps one of the big ones for me is that both are long term endeavours. I think there are fewer and fewer careers these days that really value, and rely on, the ability to focus on something for years. That kind of commitment is essential if you're going to be a scientist I think, and equally essential if you're going to write a novel. They both take deep consideration – and that means they take a lot of time. There are no easy answers or short cuts or quick rewards. But that feeling of completely immersing myself in a subject is definitely part of why I love both scientific research and writing.

Both are highly imaginative subjects too. If you want to hypothesise, or understand a new and unexpected result, or put yourself in another person's shoes, or explore the intricacies of a relationship, then you need imagination. But for both science and writing, that creative side needs to be tempered with observation, and for that to work you need a logical approach to experimentation (in the case of science) and motivation (in the case of writing). A character's behaviour has to make sense both in the context of the book and what we know about the world, just like a new scientific result or theory has to be tested and considered within the context of our existing knowledge. So I think both share that balance between a highly imaginative 'what if' and a logically observed 'what we know'.

PG: Who have been the most signficant influences on you as a writer?

HS: I've been asked this question a few times, and every time I seem to end up giving a completely different answer! I think the truth is that there are so many influences on my work it's really hard to isolate just a few. Influences that I think were important to me while writing *The Growing Season* include Ursula Le Guin's *The Left Hand of Darkness* (structurally as well as thematically) and Kazuo Ishiguro's *Never Let Me Go*, as well as the more obvious connections with Huxley's *Brave New World* and Atwood's *The Handmaid's Tale*.

Going back over the years though, my reading tastes have changed dramatically and I think I've been influenced by a range of very different authors at different times. In no particular order: Kate Atkinson, John Wyndham, Annie Proulx, Joseph Conrad, Kurt Vonnegut, Donna Tartt, Tolstoy, Jackie Kay, Vikram Seth, Angela Carter, Robert Harris, Laura Esquivel – and that's basically just the first few names that popped into my head.

Blade Runner certainly had a huge impact when I was younger (I saw the film years before reading the story) as did *The Dark Is Rising* series by Susan Cooper. I'm literally trying to force myself to stop writing now so that I don't just start listing the entire contents of my bookshelves...

But in terms of what I'm writing next, the list changes again. I've got ideas for two very different novels, both in the early stages at the moment, and the big influences I'd name right now are: Joanna Russ's *The Female Man*, *Fever Dream* by Samanta Schweblin and *The Private Lives of Trees* by Alejandro Zambra.

PG: I'm intrigued by the ways in which your books have been publicised and considered by readers. *The Comet Seekers*, in particular, wasn't really presented as an SF novel and *The Growing Season* is getting reviews in places which don't normally consider SF. Perhaps this is symbolic of the way in which SF is increasingly crossing over into mainstream fiction. Do you think of yourself as an SF author? Do you read SF?

HS: I love reading science fiction! And that goes beyond books as well, I love watching SF films, TV shows – basically given any means of storytelling we have, I think science fiction offers many of the most interesting ideas around, in the most exciting way. I'm always drawn to SF stories with underlying themes about what it means to be alive, or what we mean by things like gender, sexuality, truth, free will... I love stories that use science fiction to explore politics, technology, identity, sociology, power. In general I'm less keen on stories that heavily feature guns or lasers – in any genre, I always get bored when people start shooting at each other!

And do I think of myself as a science fiction author? I think the honest answer is

> **"given any means of storytelling we have, I think science fiction offers many of the most interesting ideas around, in the most exciting way"**

106

yes, sometimes. *The Growing Season* certainly could be described as science fiction and/or speculative fiction, whereas *The Comet Seekers* I think is more accurately described as a novel about science – it's the supernatural elements to the story, rather than the scientific ideas, that push the boundaries of reality. That said, if people want to interpret it as a type of science fiction, I'd be delighted! I enjoy leaving things up to the reader to decide. Every time I sit down to start a new novel it seems to be something totally different, but ideas from science and SF certainly provide a lot of my inspiration. For my next projects, I have plans for a horror story about a giant flower, a collaboration about a highland landscape and mythology, and a science fiction novel about quantum entanglement set on two planets across four time periods. So, a bit of a range, but there's definitely a strong science fiction thread running through it!

PG: That all sounds fantastic! One last question, we've talked about the writerly influences upon your work but are you influenced in your writing by any scientists? (Personally I love the writing of the early 20th century geneticist J.B.S. Haldane, who wrote essays and children's stories in a style that was both brilliantly clear and witty.)

HS: J.B.S. Haldane is great, and was a huge influence on *The Growing Season* – it's a book about ectogenesis, and I don't think it would have been possible to write that without being influenced by Haldane! Rosalind Franklin is mentioned in the book as well, and in my fictional world she acted as a mentor and inspiration to one of my main characters. She had a fascinating life, as well as being an exceptional scientist. As with most physicists, I think I have to mention Richard Feynman as an influence – when I was studying he seemed to embody the creative joy of science. And for *The Comet Seekers*, I was quite influenced by the thought of *all* the astronomers out there, amateur and professional. A lot of comets are still discovered by amateurs watching the sky, and I love the idea of this network of people around the world, all in different situations and countries and cultures, looking out into the solar system.

PG: Many thanks for talking to Shoreline.

Helen's website:
www.helensedgwick.com

Noise and Sparks: The Company of Bears

Ruth EJ Booth

Once upon a time – this April, in fact – a storyteller took to his blog to wonder if this year's Eastercon was "the last great convention."[1] For him, it had been a disappointing affair, not least because many of his friends had skipped the event. But mostly, his disenchantment was down to what he saw as the unfortunate absence of bears.

The blog caused no few waves.[2] Of course, there had been bears present – there always are at conventions – and the most

---

1 Adrian Faulkner, "The Last Convention? – The Climb #85," adrianfaulkner.com, http://adrianfaulkner.com/2017/04/17/the-last-convention-the-climb-85/ [accessed 19th August 2017].
2 Adrian Faulkner, "Well, That Escalated Quickly – The Climb #86," adrianfaulkner.com, http://adrianfaulkner.com/2017/04/18/well-that-escalated-quickly-the-climb-86/ [accessed 19th August 2017].

vehement objection came from one of those attending. But not because she wanted to be counted. She objected to the idea that the only reason they had spoken that weekend was for her heavy paws, her imposing stature. She had hoped, not unreasonably, that he might have appreciated her company as well.

There are many reasons why people attend cons: to discuss their favourite lore with fellow fans and scholars; to spread a little glamour in the guise of beloved heroes; or simply for the chance to visit

with kith and kin (and have a few ales on the side). For me, after five years of con-going, to attend only for the bears – at least, for their role as the champions of true story and true storytellers – would mean missing out on much of the magic of the event.

Perhaps it's the nostalgia speaking. I am, after all, typing belly-down on the floor, amidst a forest of damp laundry from Worldcon in Helsinki, breathing the evaporating spirits of scant days spent in a magical country. A Worldcon's quintessence is unique to each of us, and this year, it's a distillation of some of my favourite things: sunshine and warmth; the smell of books, cut cloth, and facepaint; the fresh tingle of fascinating new ideas; hearty meals with good friends, laughing as we stuff as many cloudberries into our mouths as we possibly can. When I lift clothes from the overflowing laundry basket, I remember sea-buckthorn, and gin, and song. I remember burning smithy tar.

I remember lightning, and the company of bears.

Blogs are full of sensible advice on how to handle bears at cons. Approach respectfully. Don't speak too loudly, or be too pushy. To consider that a bear might not be in the best of moods after three days of fierce scrapping and fraught diplomacy seems common sense, though it may not be obvious to those of us new to storytelling, excited to meet our first bears and keen to impress.

> **"It's said a scribe is simply someone who is interested in everything."**

This kind of advice evokes a certain image of bears; that of stern, no-nonsense creatures. And, certainly, there is that side to bears – it's what makes them such great champions of story. But too much of a care for this can also lead to fear of a bear's potential. Befriending a bear may be rewarding, but remember the heavy paws, those sharp teeth. A raucous night could end prematurely if they catch you with a careless claw. Whether they fight for you or no, in a world where reputation is all, how much of your fate do they hold in their paws? They aren't tame animals, after all. If you should accidentally offend a bear, what is to stop them discarding your tales for those of others – or worse, turning on you when you least expect it, and ripping your precious work apart?

It is easy to forget this is not all that bears are.

This kind of advice was utmost in my mind when I started going to conventions. But the more panels I sat in, the more workshops I attended, the more I came to realize that these events are about more than just strategy and alliances. A single corridor might hold talks and tastings, demonstrations, classes, performances and plays. Where else can we discover the deep structure of universes in the morning, knit their complex manifolds in the afternoon, and shape their stars into jewellery in the evening? It's said a scribe is simply someone who is interested in everything. Conventions are one of the few places where you can explore this idea to its fullest extent.

Moreover, a convention is a place to grow and explore alongside other fans of the fantastic. A chance to be with those who share our passion and enthusiasm for story in all its forms. Whether they're company for the afternoon, or potential friends for life, it's a chance to step away from it all with folks who understand. Here is where the real magic of conventions lies, and it lingers long after the memory of panels on ursine diplomacy or talks on battlefield tactics. They're the things that bind us all together. And that includes bears.

See, bears don't begin as warriors. Some were scholars,

lorekeepers, magicians – yes, even storytellers. Many still are: their bearhood makes them no less so. For the love of the stories that drew us to the craft is the same love that leads them to champion those tales. While conventions are undoubtedly useful places of negotiation and combat, the magic of community is just as much a draw for bears as any of us. Some of the best times I've had at cons have been with bears, whether at karaoke, discussing the intricacies of lore at the bar, or disco dancing.

Bears should always be respected. But perhaps this respect should be no different from that we'd afford anyone else in our community – to consider their boundaries and personal spaces. Why should we not, in essence, respect bears for their whole selves, as fantastic creatures in their own right? Talk of "handling" bears is intended as caution against foolishness, but respect and fear are not equivalencies. Surely, in the end, respecting bears for themselves not only leads to healthier, more productive working relationships, but a more welcoming community for us all, wherever we're lucky enough to find it.

There are undoubtedly scribes for whom this approach works. There will be bards who say their fondest memories of Helsinki are hands shaken, vows cast, and battlefield alliances made. These are valuable and worthy things. Me? I'll pick the cloudberry out of my teeth, brush the soot from my clothes. I'll smile, and remember the company of bears.

Ruth EJ Booth is a BSFA Award-winning bard, lorekeeper, bear-friend, and now bear, based in Glasgow, Scotland. For more tales and ballads, head to www.ruthbooth.com – or for those of others, see www.glasgowtosaturn.com

Reviews

Too Light The Lightning
Ada Palmer
Tor, 432 pages
Review by Eris Young

It is the year 2454, and the invention of flying cars has long since made geographical borders, and, by extension, nations, obsolete: if you live in Chile but work in Japan and have dinner in France, what does it matter what country you were born in? Instead, people choose from a selection of seven global governments based on their interests and ideals. The nuclear family has been replaced by a larger family unit that you choose yourself. The average life expectancy is over one hundred and trips to the moon are government-subsidised.

But there is also a universal tracker system that makes hiding from the government largely impossible, censorship is rife and any discussion of metaphysics or religion is strictly regulated. The world of Ada Palmer's *Too Like the Lightning* is at once surveillance state and utopia, the dream of a fevered political scientist. Into this mix we add a vast conspiracy with world-shaking implications, and a boy who can perform miracles.

Though the implications of his power are not fully explored in the first book, the existence of young Bridger – who can bring toys to life (and *back* to life), and create from simple drawings 'healing potions' to cure any ailment – might pose a problem in a world that 'has no need for religion'. Protected fiercely by narrator Canner, and gradually more aware of the potential of his power, Bridger risks exhaustion and enslavement for the 'greater good' if the government get wind of him. Bridger's narrative forms the emotional hook, and bookends the story, the bulk of which deals with developing the conspiracy storyline in parallel. Bridger rounds out the story nicely but I couldn't help wondering if his existential implications were a bit of a stretch; surely 'miracles' are only a threat to secular society if they cannot, in fact, be explained by science?

It's one thing to build an inventive world that immerses the reader, and an entire other to craft a good story within that world. Palmer has succeeded at both, but it takes a while for that to become apparent. The story is written in an archaic and rather florid style, apparently after the French enlightenment (but, you know, in English), and narrated by Mycroft Canner, an ex-con and slave of the state, a statusless 'servicer'. Canner's prose is flowery and, ostensibly for the benefit of a future reader unfamiliar with his world, every scene and custom and gesture is lovingly described, so much so that it was halfway through the book before any conflict was introduced.

So the book is worldbuilding-heavy, as many of the best sci-fi novels are. But as I read I couldn't help getting the sense that Palmer may have tried to do slightly too much. In particular, I found the way the story approaches language and gender a bit implausible. Though the prose is in English, the characters themselves speak many different languages, indicated in dialogue by the quotation marks conventionally used in those languages. So far, so realistic, but for the fact that there is also a prohibition on using gendered language to describe another person. No 'he', 'she', 'man', 'daughter', 'wife' etc, for anyone, no matter what government they belong to or language they use.

The problem with this is that every language uses gender differently. Some have only third person pronouns and nouns that are semantically but not

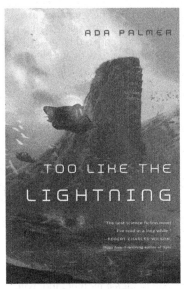

grammatically gendered, like English. Others, like the romance languages, gender just about every thing you could name. In Japanese, gender is expressed in the first person but not the third (in fact, referring to someone else using a second- or third-person pronoun at all is considered a bit rude). In some languages there is already a neutral pronoun and in some there is no way to remove gender without inventing an entire new declension and several new lexemes. Basically, it's a lot easier to ban someone from talking about God than it is to invent an entire new language.

From a pragmatic perspective this type of censorship seems impossible to enforce and would probably involve way more effort than it was worth. Even if you view it as more of a thought experiment and don't worry about the practicalities, you begin to wonder how it would have come about. Is the implication that it is "PC culture" gone mad? Is

Palmer's point here to show us how silly and impossible trying to regulate gendered language is? In a universe with attributes of both utopias – and dystopias, it's hard to see where gendered censorship is supposed to lie.

Too Like the Lightning is Clever with a capital 'C': the author has hit upon a concept and drawn it out to the fullest possible extent. Canner often addresses the reader directly, pre-empting questions that I, at least, would not have asked. At one point he describes a character with facial stubble as 'she', and forestalls our objections by saying he'd seen the character protect a child 'with a mother's ferocity'. Setting aside the sexism (the book is full of 'fierce mother' and 'witch' tropes which the imagined reader rails against, and which Canner rationalises but does not fully justify) this assumption completely ignores the fact that some women *do* have facial hair. This implies that social progress and linguistic censorship might make transgender people, as it were, obsolete. Since the narrator directly addresses the reader, we are forced into tacit acceptance of a view which I, as transgender, found insulting.

Too Like the Lightning is without a doubt worth a read. It's inventive and, like all the best sci-fi, challenges our current status quo. It shows us a future that is (if a little optimistic) not totally outside the realm of possibility, and it creates a plausible conflict that keeps the reader guessing until the end. Palmer draws on literature, science, classics and philosophy to create a beautifully written 'future history'. But I'd advise approaching with a critical eye, lest you be blinded to its faults by fancy tech and pretty language.

Infinity Wars
Jonathan Strahan (Editor)
Rebellion, 356 pages
Reviewed by Ian Hunter

It was inevitably, I suppose, given that the previous five entries in Jonathan Strahan's *Infinity Project* – at least from their titles – had a hopeful air about them starting way back in 2010 with *Engineering Infinity* right through to more recent offerings, that things would take a turn for the worse. So in book six, we have reached *Infinity Wars*. War is eternal, and one thing that mankind can always be counted on is its ability to be creative when waging it. I couldn't help recalling the late great American writer, historian and commentator, Gore Vidal, saying that the American economy always needed a good war from time to time to kickstart employment, investment and innovation. Some of these stories perhaps share Vidal's cynicism in depicting the lengths that the military, big business and even the government will go to win, or make money, or manipulate their populace into thinking that what they are doing is right.

Strahan, ever the consummate anthologist and editor brings together a variety of stories from writers who are either well-known to science fiction readers, such as Elizabeth Bear, Garth Nix, Peter Watts and Aliette deBodard; or are writers who are less familiar, but they all share one thing in common – they can all tell a tale. Often that tale isn't what you would expect in that it is not a straightforward military science fiction tale. One reads like a murder mystery, one is about the supply side of war, two are set in post-climate change futures, one might even be called

"Full Metal Jacket with Zombies", while others featuring AIs, and a couple are deep, multi-layered tales that require a re-reread. All of that should offer a clue to any prospective reader that many of these are stories are character driven, revealing the effect that war has on the central character or their families and friends.

In his introduction, Strahan muses that war has changed and is no longer as straight-forward as a simple country versus country affair. For me, the game changer was the first Gulf War, which was covered almost live by the BBC, showing cities being bombarded as the night sky blossomed into reds and oranges, which actually meant that buildings were being destroyed and people were being killed. We had briefings by military personnel standing in front of screens showing targets being obliterated from above. Now, the waters are muddied by drone strikes, invaders, insurgents, terrorism, and collateral damage; and the fifteen stories gathered here take several different aspects of the 'war machine' and extrapolated them into the future.

An anthology is always going to have some hit and miss stories, depending on the taste of the reader, but there are some stand out stories inspired by highly original ideas such as in Caroline M. Yoachim's *Faceless Soldiers, Patchwork Ships* where a soldier is modified to look like the enemy in order to infiltrate their ship. However, the catch is that if she doesn't complete her mission in time she won't be able to be restored to her true form and will remain looking like the enemy. A total change of tact, and very funny too, is Garth Nix's

Conversations with an Armoury where soldiers at an isolated outpost are facing an imminent attack. If only the soldiers can open the nearby armoury and get to the weapons inside they might have a chance of survival, but the route is controlled by an AI that is a stickler for the rules, and getting in isn't going to be as easy as it seems. AIs also feature in *Perfect Gun* by Elizabeth Bear, where a mercenary buys a war machine with an AI for a brain, and while their relationship grows, perhaps the AI running the ship has more morals than the human who owns it. Relationships are also at the fore in *Mines*, a story which focusses on characters who clear mines. We experience a growing sense of trust, reliance and (possibly) love between the characters, one of whom isn't human. The use of information features in two stories: *The Last Broadcasts* by An Owomoyela, where the truth has to be concealed and altered for the so-called greater good. But if you know about the lie, how will it effect you, and what can you do about it? In E. J. Swift's *Weather Girl*, information about weather systems is being withheld from the enemy to allow storms to become weapons.

Other aspects of war range from the use of predictive software through occupying alien worlds, to the effect of war on the survivors and their families. The anthology ends with a bang in Peter Watts' lengthy tale, *ZeroS*, where humans are resurrected and upgraded to become weapons. They are tested on missions that make them question what they have become, what it means to be human, and how far they are willing to go to become human again.

All in all, file *Infinity Wars* under 'r' for recommended

New York 2140
Kim Stanley Robinson
Orbit, 618 pages
Review by Callum McSorley

New York, New York, it's a helluva town! So goes the song, and from Paul Auster's *New York Trilogy* to Fitzgerald's *The Great Gatsby*, it's certainly a city that's inspired writers and artists for generations, and its prominence in media and finance has made it the capital of the world. Even over a hundred years in the future, where melting polar ice caps have caused worldwide floods and left half of Manhattan under water – the premise of Kim Stanley Robinson's *New York 2140* – the great city of New York is still a thriving metropolis, setting the bar for all the so-called 'intertidal' cities of the world.

This is *not* a post-apocalyptic story. Manhattan may be in the drink, but hardy New Yorkers simply get on with it, traversing the new canals in ferries and souped-up speedboats, farming fresh fish and seafood in the streets and avenues downtown, and attending water-sumo wrestling matches in the illicit subterranean drinking dungeons in the former subway. The book follows a group of such folk who all live in the Met Life building on Madison Square in the heart of the 'SuperVenice'.

New York 2140 is overtly political, wearing its ideas on environmentalism and the economy on its sleeve, and in many places it's a straight critique of the 2008 crash, openly lambasting the bail out of the banks and the return to the status quo of high finance gambling. The main plot point involves a similar crash predicted by Wall Street trader Franklin Garr (his Patrick Bateman persona hiding the fact that he's really a do-gooder at heart) who joins up with a rag tag group of coders, counsellors, politicians, bureaucrats and water rats to change the future. (All of them happen to live in the same building – a fact brought to the reader's attention by Robinson himself in a knowing bit of metafiction.)

The characters are diverse – reflecting the mongrel nature of the city itself – and boast strong female leads in Claire Armstrong, who spends her time finding homes for the city's many immigrants and is tired of the indifference of the rich and political classes, and NYPD inspector, Gen Octaviasdottir, a former water sumo and old-school cop who lives and breathes the force's motto of 'protect and serve'.

Despite a couple of near-drownings and a deadly hurricane that batters the city, *New York 2140* is relentlessly upbeat, with characters rarely unable to quickly overcome problems, something which weakens the thriller elements of the plot (two coders – Mutt and Jeff – are kidnapped at the beginning of the tale and somebody is drilling holes in the Met Life building in an act of sabotage) that largely fade out.

Another weak point is some of Robinson's anachronistic twentieth-century pop culture references that seem odd coming from the mouths of people living over a century in the future. Likewise, interludes by 'The Citizen' break up the plot with snarky-toned discussions of New York's past both real and fictional (in the years between now and 2142 when the book is set) are sometimes genuinely interesting but other times are just large information

dumps – 'The Citizen' even jokes that you should skip these if you simply want to get back to your little story, and you might just want to take his advice on occasion.

New York 2140 is about the present. It's about the climate change we're currently causing and ignoring. It's about the growing inequality between rich and poor – above Central Park, still on dry land, there are 'superscrapers' lying empty, owned by the rich as holiday homes or as investments. It's a call for action and reform, a speculation on communal living, and, most of all, a vibrant love letter to the city of New York.

This last is the most important factor, and whether you're digging for buried gold in the old underwater streets in a home-made diving bell with water rats Stefan and Roberto, or taking in the famous skyline of the sunken city in a swish open-terrace bar with Franklin, it's a joy to be in New York in 2140.

The Death and Life of Schneider Wrack
by Nate Crowley
Abaddon, 400 pages
Review by S-J McGeachy

When a book's prologue consists of quotations from Samuel Taylor Coleridge and Eric Morecombe you hope for a healthy combination of grim despair and hearty chuckles. Thankfully, Nate Crowley delivers both in spades.

Schneider Wrack regains consciousness and slowly becomes aware that he is dead. His corpse has been reanimated so he can serve at sea, carrying out the tasks the living would really rather not. Having been executed for political dissension, he now finds himself aboard a megaship factory. His workmates comprise former military personnel, criminals and subversives, all of whom are as dead as he is. Horrified by the injustice of the situation and the society which condones it, Wrack heads up a zombie insurrection. First he must rouse his comrades from their post-death indifference.

This could easily devolve into clumsy political metaphor were it not for the nuances and complexity of Crowley's writing. In a recent move away from the groaning brain-munchers of Romero movies, M. R. Carey's *The Girl with All the Gifts* has set the bench mark for sentient zombie novels. In a very different, but equally effective way *The Life and Death of Schneider Wrack* also manages to breathe new life into this undead subject matter. The story is broken down into two distinct sections which were originally published as two separate novellas. There are moments where the story is in danger of losing itself in a confused, surrealist soup – particularly in the second section. However, the skill of the writer just about prevents this. Strong characters and meticulous world building anchor the events in their own bizarre logic.

The wonderful use of language is one of this book's greatest strengths; it is also one of its most understated attributes. The historical and mythological nomenclature walks a clever tightrope between the strange and the familiar. Crowley also engenders a sickening authenticity to the war-weary society and the effects of systemic conflict. To escape the increasing horror,

'Genius.'
Dara Ó Briain
on Nate Crowley

THE DEATH AND LIFE OF SCHNEIDER WRACK

NATE CROWLEY

Wrack loses himself in the beloved travel journals of his childhood. The tone of these encyclopaedic entries lies somewhere between *Moby Dick* and *The Hitchhikers Guide to the Galaxy*.

In the latter part of the story primary focus switches from Wrack to Mouana – a fellow zombie rebel. Her military past comes back to her in flashes of brutality and regret. Now is her chance to complete the unfinished business she has with the barbaric General Dust. The relationship between the two female soldiers, Mouana and Dust, is deeply refreshing mainly because their gender is not an issue in this world. They are simply well-drawn characters displaying a range of human and inhuman reactions.

There are many other supporting characters who add texture and colour to the narrative. Most notably The Bruiser, whose stilted journey back to self-awareness confines his speech to a single profanity. His attempts at finding subtlety in this one phrase provide some genuinely funny moments. Although, some readers have taken issue with the blurb's description of the novel as a comedy, Crowley's wit is always present to cut through the bleakness of the circumstances.

Arguably there are unresolved plot points, but this left me craving a sequel, so perhaps that's not such a bad thing. In the postscript Daniel Baker touches on some interesting possibilities surrounding narrative creation on social media and it feels as though there maybe untapped potential here. This book is not going to float everybody's zombie-crewed boat, but if you're willing to resign yourself to the sheer weirdness of the ride, then there is much to enjoy.

2084

George Sandison (Editor)
Unsung Stories, 344 pages
Review by Marija Smits

2084 came into being through a highly successful Kickstarter campaign. The blurb on the back states:

"15 predictions of the world, 67 years in the future. These stories envision what our world could become."

And yet in the Introduction, editor George Sandison writes:

This isn't a book about the future... This isn't a book of predictions... This isn't a book of Orwellian stories.

So what can the reader expect from an anthology that's inspired by the centenary of the infamous, science fictional year 1984 and yet claims to *not* be a book of predictions? Well, they can expect an engaging collection of dystopian short stories by talented writers.

Sandison has done a fine job of ordering the stories in the collection; he's got a good understanding of how (if read in order) the stories play off each other, and has shown sensitivity in this challenging and often unacknowledged task. However, when crafting their dystopias most of the writers have used the same technique: to zoom in on one facet of our present lives and to then extrapolate in a linear fashion to 2084. This simple tweaking of today's reality has led to many of the stories being small in scope, and tending more to the literary side of literary science fiction. The majority are based in the western world, giving a rather one-sided picture.

The most successful stories are those that more fully investigate the 'why?' and 'how?' of the future; in many of these stories the issue of boundaries is a key theme. For instance: in the strong opening story, *Babylon*, Dave Hutchinson has his protagonist slip into Europe, past the heavily patrolled borders, with a curious weapon of mass destruction. Hutchinson also touches on the future's still present invisible barriers between humans of different skin colour.

Desirina Boskovich's excellent *Here Comes the Flood* is about boundaries too: between those who live in the surviving cities and those adrift in the outside, watery world. Her characters are drawn with great depth; this story was one of the strongest of the collection because it

2084

married convincing worldbuilding with good characterization.

Ian Hocking's bleak take on the future made for a compelling – if harrowing – read. In *Fly Away, Peter* the boundary between the totalitarian government's ruling and the individual's free will is very blurred. In Anne Charnock's story, *A Good Citizen* the boundaries are actual walls; she also introduces the neat idea of frequent online voting – exploring the individual's wrestle between informed and uninformed choice.

In *The Endling Market* E.J. Swift, refreshingly, considers the future fate of wild animals – 'endlings' – which are much prized for their near-magical properties (just like now, there are few protective barriers enabling the survival of other species). And Oliver Langmead's *Glitterati* is a much-needed and welcome 'lighter' story, with a grotesque though compelling protagonist. Langmead shows us that there

are no boundaries between the individual and art, creating a really satisfying piece with a proper beginning, middle and end (something that not all of the stories managed to do).

In *The Infinite Eye* JP Smythe deftly explores the crumbling borders between virtual reality, surveillance and the unemployed, producing a compelling and sympathetic story.

March, April, May by Malcolm Devlin is an enjoyable piece, and one that any current user of social media can relate to. It also centres on the theme of borders, for The Space – Devlin's bigger and more insinuating version of Facebook – is apparently "Borderless." Devlin's characterization is excellent (Billy K a wonderful addition), and in what could otherwise have been a collection of hope-free dystopias, this story interjects some much-needed leavening (although if you think about it too much, it'll make your heart hurt).

With echoes of Philip K Dick, Lavie Tidhar's *2084 Satoshi AD* is a satisfying and image-rich story in which the boundaries between individuals' genomes are blurred.

Although one of the few authors to take on the challenge of using the short story form to explore the future from a global perspective, Courttia Newland's *Percepi* wasn't wholly convincing. The story drifts from Earth to the Moon and back, via the "Buddies" – robots that are "*More human than humankind*". This last phrase is just too close to *Bladerunner*'s "more human than human" which jolted me out of the story and inevitably draws parallels. Newland is to be admired for taking on the challenge, but ultimately, the 'whys?' of the story aren't fully explored.

Overall, *2084* makes for a good read (pretty much anything Unsung Stories publishes is a good read), and I'd recommend it to anyone who wants an introduction to contemporary science fiction, or who enjoys dystopian fiction. But does it paint a convincing vision of 2084? No. There's simply not enough that's innovative here. No piece really stretched me and made me go 'wow' with its ability to turn my thinking upside down like the visionary *1984* did. But perhaps that was always going to be too much of a tall order, the connection to Orwell too much of a burden.

The Clockwork Dynasty: A Novel
Daniel H. Wilson
Doubleday, 352 pages
Review By Benjamin Thomas

Good science fiction gives us an entertaining thrill ride through a possible future, past, or present that is somehow altered, perhaps through new technologies or different ideologies. Great science fiction does the above, while asking thematic questions that resonate with both society as a whole and each reader individually. By that standard, *The Clockwork Dynasty* is great science fiction.

The Clockwork Dynasty follows parallel story lines being told in vastly different time periods. In the present day, June Stefanov, is an anthropologist working with ancient technologies, whose life and career take an unexpected spin into dangerous territory when she discovers a secret lying in an ancient mechanical doll. She finds herself being tracked and hunted, pushing her to run farther into this under ground world, headquartered (at least a little) in modern day Seattle.

The second storyline begins in 1725 Russia, following a life-like mechanical being, Peter and his younger sister Elena, both known as avtomat. The two escape Russia after Elena is taken hostage by a group of riders, and settle into a cramped and dirty London. As they attempt to fit into the human world, we find ourselves relating to these two inhuman characters because they are facing the same existential questions that you or I would in our lives. Where do we fit in? How do we know where we belong?

Each chapter alternates between these story lines. While some readers might find the constant switching back and forth distracting, I personally thought it added to the story. Wilson kept us in each character's perspective long enough to progress the plot, while not allowing us to get complacent or bored. Aside from that, Wilson's ability to distinguish between characters via actions and dialogue truly helped to individualize each of the players in *The Clockwork Dynasty*.

Overall the novel was excellent, and it explored some deep thematic questions while keeping tensions high and the pacing consistent throughout. At certain points, the science fiction elements take a backseat, however I think that they are present enough to fulfill every readers urge for great science fiction.

Multiverse

The Woman who Married the International Space Station

I'll be honest. At first
it was mostly postcode envy.
I wanted that room with a view, so I married
up. Way up. And what a view he gave me;
the blue planet's polished glass and the moon
shining in the black like a solitaire ring.

I grew attached. The way he held me
like breath. The way he spun me close
to the nickel-bright sun, spun me
like lambswool flexed around its spindle,
like silk cocoons or like a web,
the way he spooled me out.

Soon I was dizzy. Flush as the honey
moon's gold light at his window.
Ready to let my muscles waste.
By the time he rose
like a sun over the continents
I loved him like gravity.

Rachel Plummer

Production

At the city's edge the road takes you by the hand
and leads you to the factory
where children are made.

Miniature, injection moulded hands.
The perfect glass-blown spheres of heads
lining conveyor belts.
The tiny buttons of their teeth.
Their resin-fixed smiles.
The almost translucent new skin
hanging in sheets
waiting to be laid over small muscles,
clockwork hearts, fibreglass
doll skeletons.

You pick a brown glass eye
from a crate of brown glass eyes.

Held up in your hand, you notice
the way it prisms the light, sends rainbows
hopscotching onto the factory walls, how it illuminates
the machinery's clumsy crank and turn,
the gears and sprockets
in their endless music box circles.

The finished children stack themselves
end to end in metal shipping containers.

One of them, you notice, is staring
one-eyed at the eye in your hand.

Rachel Plummer

Sunday morning paradigm swap

It's so close, you could wake melting
eyelids to light on the grocery bags, still split
open from last night. That much closer to a cold star.

Except, that hand which used to count each star
would now be your other hand. And each melting
clock on the mantelpiece reminds us that you split

open time, just for one night. Now, in this star-rise, they split
apart the shells that trapped dense truths like neutron stars,
while the statues they built in their own honour are melting

like the butter sun as you split those truths melting between stars
splayed like fingers.

Jo-Ella Sarich

Rachel Plummer is a poet living in Edinburgh with her partner and two
young children. Her first solo pamphlet, *The Parlour Guide to Exo-Politics*, will
be published by House Press in late 2017. She has had poems in magazines
including *The Dark Horse and Agenda*. She is a recipient of the Scottish Book Trust
New Writers Award for poetry.

Jo-Ella Sarich is a lawyer, writer, and mother. Her poems have appeared in a
number of print and online publications, including *The New Verse News, Cleaver
Magazine, New Statesman, The Galway Review, Barzakh Magazine, Quarterday
Review, The Rising Phoenix Review, takahē magazine* and the *Poetry New Zealand
Yearbook 2017*. @jsarich_writer.

Rosemary Badcoe is designer and editor of the online poetry
journal *Antiphon*, www.antiphon.org.uk These poems were previously published
in her first collection, *Drawing a Diagram* (Kelsay Press, 2017) which is available
from http://antiphon.org.uk/rb/?p=148

The Happiest Thought and the nightmare that follows it

"The observer, therefore, is justified in interpreting his state as being 'at rest'."
- Albert Einstein

Forget the aurora ... someone whispered

above
the roar of stasis and the shudder
in empty flesh. Someone
beyond the final settling of light's debt
to matter; someone
who looked like me. When I daydreamed of

two boys,
adjacent to one another, dropping balls
to greet the concrete and laughing
at the lightning dancing
between their fingers. The strangeness
in the yield of their skin
to the other's touch. A girl asking her father
if the sky would crack like an egg. When scientists
continued to predict food shortages,
and in the dusk of daylight, crops continued
to burn. When people started turning
up at the doors of their public libraries
seeking answers about the unbirth
of stars. I sat up

on the mattress of strange matter and my hand
passed through the slurry of the falling phosphor clock
as you continued dreaming. I felt odd at the thought
of my own immortality. There is

a butterfly outside my window, flickering under
the ceiling fan like the entropy
in our connection. At that same moment, many people
started believing me. Forget Mars, I said,
as the lights were snuffed like electrons
from the sky, and the second hand moved
irresistibly to nul. There is one ball
of infinite matter at our centre and one beyond
the firewall, striking
against its concrete shell. Tell your finite
selves to hear the roar of the Void now.
Follow the flicker of
light that runs
frantically in the opposite direction.

Jo-Ella Sarich

Mars

This world turned its back on life,
subsumed its water into rock, let oxygen
drift up beyond the mountain's shoulder.
Rocks slammed the surface, splashed plumes
that grasped the air and swept it
into space. Now sublimated ice
drifts as a ghost from pole to pole,
whispers nothing of its journey
but the sputtering of solar winds,
the gentle weight of entropy
spreading a silence, fine and cool.

Curiosity

The rover's shadow is our own.

First you photograph yourself, the rock,
and as the grainy black and white
resolves into an image
three hundred million miles re-forms
to fourteen minutes. Strung on your arms
our senses piggy-back, a spider-silk
of optic nerve stretched past our planet's end.
This scoop, this tiny drill, are fingernails
that scratch a reddened land.
Shadows cast by rolled titanium
take on a human form.

SETI

We spend our days collecting worlds
lost in the hum of sunbeams,
thumbs hung out to catch the light
bent through the lens of gravity.
We cannot shake the damp
off limbs evolved from fins
to kick the dryness of an alien dust.
We're tethered like a buoy,
signposting *mostly conscious*
in a cosmos where the shipping lanes
are curiously parched.

Rosemary Badcoe

Parabolic Puzzles
Name that Author

At Event Horizon on Wednesday 7th November 2017, Shoreline's own Master Puzzler Paul Holmes enthralled the members of the audience with his mastery of the brain teaser. At the break he handed them a picture quiz.

Feverishly, they worked away, brains gnashing, teeth straining. The winning team managed 17 out of 18, and were amply rewarded with a bag of sweets to share.

You too can test your knowledge of science fiction authors past and present. Can you beat the team at Event Horizon?

You have until **midnight 28th February 2018** to get your entries in to the contact form on our websiteat

www.shorelineofinfinity.com/contact

If you score 18 out of 18 we will drop your name into the Shoreline Hat, and the winner will receive a 1 year digital subscription to *Shoreline of Infinity Science Fiction Magazine*.

Go to it!

—*Editor*

	1. He wrote of walking plants and waking monsters.		2. Daughter of an advocate for women's rights.
	3. In 1995 she became the first science fiction writer to receive the MacArthur Fellowship.		4. He fostered the development of the Sci-Fi New Wave

	5. He died in Oxford this August		6 .Multi-award winning New York author, holder of 17 doctorates.
	7. Associate professor in creative writing at University of California.		8. Quote "I love deadlines. I like the whooshing sound they make as they fly by."
	9. Most famous works were inspired by a geographical feature in Oregon.		10. She submitted her first story to Astounding Science Fiction at age 11.
	11. Published as a man from 1967 to her death 20 years later. (Either her real name or pen name will do.)		12. American writer, interned in Dresden during WWII.
	13. Died in Colombo		14. First name Herbert

	15. Born in Nantes		16. Professor born in Petrovichi, Smolensk Oblast, Russia.
	17. 282.8 degrees Celsius		18. Middle name Kindred

Paul's latest collection of Puzzles, *The Galactic Festival* is published by Shoreline of Infinity Publications.
Available from www.shorelineofinfinity.com and from bookshops worldwide.

HOW TO SUPPORT SCOTLAND'S SCIENCE FICTION MAGAZINE

BECOME A PATRON

SHORELINE OF INFINITY HAS A PATREON PAGE AT

WWW.PATREON.COM/ SHORELINEOFINFINITY

ON PATREON, YOU CAN PLEDGE A MONTHLY PAYMENT FROM AS LOW AS $1 IN EXCHANGE FOR A COOL TITLE AND A REGULAR REWARD.

ALL PATRONS GET AN EARLY DIGITAL ISSUE OF THE MAGAZINE QUARTERLY AND EXCLUSIVE ACCESS TO OUR PATREON MESSAGE FEED AND SOME GET A LOT MORE. HOW ABOUT THESE?

POTENT PROTECTOR SPONSORS A STORY EVERY YEAR WITH FULL CREDIT IN THE MAGAZINE WHILE AN AWESOME AEGIS SPONSORS AN ILLUSTRATION.

TRUE BELIEVER SPONSORS A BEACHCOMBER COMIC AND MIGHTY MENTOR SPONSORS A COVER PICTURE.

AND .... OUR HIGHEST HONOUR ... SUPREME SENTINEL SPONSORS A WHOLE ISSUE OF SHORELINE OF INFINITY.

CONER '17

ASK YOUR FAVOURITE BOOK SHOP TO GET YOU A COPY. WE ARE ON THE TRADE DISTRIBUTION LISTS.

OR BUY A COPY DIRECTLY FROM OUR ONLINE SHOP AT

WWW.SHORELINEOFINFINITY.COM

YOU CAN GET AN ANNUAL SUBSCRIPTION THERE TOO.

KINDLE FANS CAN GET SHORELINE FROM THE AMAZON KINDLE STORE.

The story continues...

www.shorelineofinfinity.com

Lightning Source UK Ltd.
Milton Keynes UK
UKOW06f1344251117
313314UK00005B/206/P